WYLDBLOOD
MAGAZINE

Contents

Welcome to the fourth issue of Wyldblood Magazine – once more packed with great stories to delight, chill and inspire. We've got Mark Rigney's *Taming Dash Nine*, with its unlikely alliance of freedom fighters and security robot nightmares, Carol Gore's *Extraordinary Lessons for Startling Success,* a chilling tale of ruthless remorselessness, and Naomi Vondell's *The Road to Shambala,* where the planet of the spiders puts us firmly in our place.

Natalie Dale's *Snakeflower* is a satisfying tale of sweet smelling revenge on a colony world where protectors turn oppressor, Alexandra Grunberg's *To the New Year* takes us to the end of the world, and Tova Hope Liel, *Girl's Best Friend* asks: is the monster under the bed real? And if it is, does it bite?

Matias Travieso-Diaz's **The Portal** is a cautionary tale of demons summoned, pacts made and consequences suffered. Shawn Kobb's *Two by Two* shows coexisting with aliens might not be straightforward and, finally,. David Dixon's *Seventy Miles from Phoenix* ladles death and destruction in the Arizona desert.

Fine fantasy and stunning science fiction. Enjoy.

Publisher:
Wyldblood Press,
Thicket View, Bakers Lane,
Maidenhead
SL6 6PX UK

Editor: Mark Bilsborough
Fiction editor Sandra Baker
First readers:
Vaughan Stanger
Mike Lewis
Rebecca Ruvinsky

Subscriptions: 6 issues epub/mobi/pdf delivered to your inbox £15.
6 issue print subscriptions £35
www.wyldblood.com/magazine.

Single issues available worldwide via Amazon and from Wyldblood.

www.wyldblood.com
contact@wyldblood.com
facebook.com/WyldbloodPress
t: @WyldbloodPress

Submissions: we are regularly open for submissions for flash fiction, short stories and novels – check our website for our current status and requirements. We are a paying market.

Issue 5 available to pre-order now – published September 2021
www.wyldblood.com/magazine

We need people to review us, and people to review *for* us. Email mark@wyldblood.com

ISBN: 978-1-914417-03-0

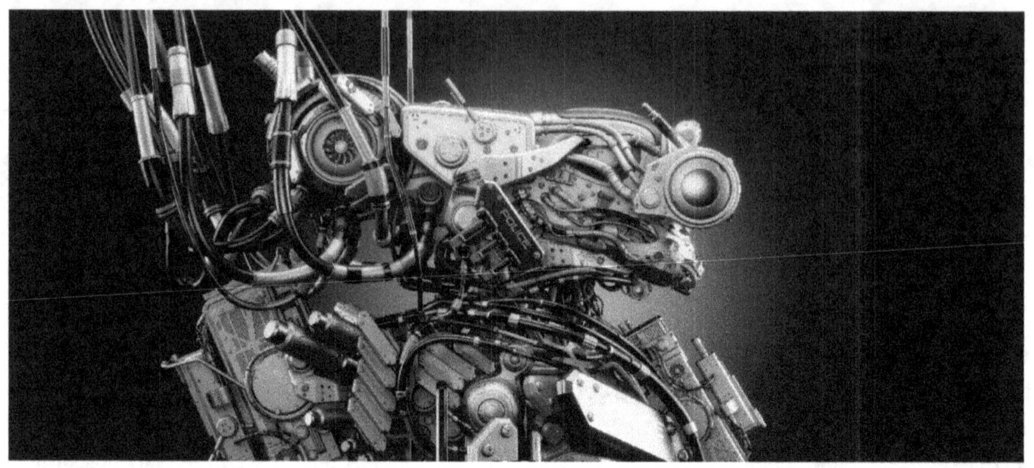

Taming Dash Nine
Mark Rigney

First off, can we get one thing straight? I'm a freedom fighter, not a terrorist. Second, we knew perfectly well that we'd attract the attention of a Centaur-7, and thereby hangs a tale.

Liam and I hadn't been in the Whitmore house for even twenty minutes before the Centaur clanked up the driveway and rapped its powerful alloy knuckles on the towering front door. We answered promptly, because that was expected, and if Liam's phone hadn't already been jamming the Centaur's visuals (with his very own custom-designed app, no less), that bot would have seen two medium-height, deliberately unremarkable, theoretically-but-not-actually Caucasian persons in light gray delivery coveralls, harmless service techs out to refurbish a cranky dishwasher in a lily-white neighborhood. What it saw instead is anyone's guess, since that app was hurling interference like a sandstorm flinging dust.

Now, I'm not gonna lie. The Centaur-7 is an exceptional neighborhood security device, proof positive that action really is eloquence. They've got four strong legs for speed and fence-clearing leaps, plus a muscular humanoid torso; the two long arms terminate in a pair of hands with dexterous fingers and opposable thumbs. Hidden under its various body panels, it carries an extraordinary arsenal of lethal weaponry. Only the head, squat and multi-planar, disappoints. It looks like an old outboard motor. I'm not even sure what it's for, except to house the speaker for its surprisingly resonant baritone voice. Liam claims this was an intentional ruse on the part of its New Confederation designers, an open invitation to waste your time shooting at the head when all its major sensory systems lurk elsewhere.

My point is that standing so close to a Centaur-7 is usually a recipe for certain and sudden death, but we'd tried Liam's interference trick before, first in Louisville and again in Tulsa, so we had good reason to believe we'd survive the encounter. Our role now was to be seen as legitimate appliance repair techs, the kind that would clearly blanche in the face of an inquisitive Centaur-7. It was also crucial that our facial features not be uploaded, scanned, and matched. Hence, our green-tinted contact lenses, my frizzy wig, and Liam's crumb catcher of a false mustache. Between these old-school parlor tricks and Liam's jamming app, we felt fairly confident that we had both household security and the Centaur foxed.

"Please confirm your purpose and presence," the Centaur said.

"We got a call to service a dishwasher," I replied, which was perfectly true. It was also perfectly true that we'd been waiting months for one of the Whitmore home's systems to go on the fritz so we could intercept the work order, then install listening devices. The fact that it was the dishwasher that had gone belly up was beyond our wildest hopes. Who thinks to look for listening devices in a dishwasher? Starting today, and except for those brief moments when the machine was actually running, we'd be pulling in every conversation within a forty-foot radius.

The Centaur whirred and fidgeted. Its head cocked to one side, dog-like. It was still working through various subroutines to try and clear its vision. At last it said, "Confirm your identification, please."

Like a dutiful school child, I held out the barcoder disc we'd been given at the compound's main gate. Simple things, lumpy and palm-sized, barcoder discs are designed for scanning visitors in and then out of any semi-secure setting. We use them on our side of the border, too.

At the same moment, Liam switched off his app and we both looked at our shoes. This gave the Centaur-7 a clear chance to read the barcoder with no interference. Yes, we were indeed the same two service techs who had been cleared at the gate, and we matched nicely to the cargo van we'd parked at the curb.

"Are there additional persons in the house?" the Centaur asked, as it returned the barcoder.

"Just us," I said, as Liam switched his app back on.

"Have you finished your repair?"

We had not. Liam and I are excellent covert field operatives, but dishwashers? Not our specialty. The crash course we'd undertaken over the past thirty-six hours had allowed us to extract Supply Chief Tiber Whitmore's busted heating element with relative ease, but we were some distance from installing its replacement. Besides, we'd spent the first ten minutes getting our microphone mounted. Priorities.

I explained to the Centaur that we were still diagnosing the problem, and the robot's head nodded as if considering the idea (a slick piece of programming, that; very human). At last, it said, "You expect to resolve the situation shortly."

"Just waiting on the right inspiration."

Now, I'm a big girl, so I can admit right here and right now that that was a stupid thing to say. Diagnostics and experience, that's what service techs are supposed to rely on, especially when addressing a very literal, security-minded robot. Worse, this wasn't one of the responses we'd rehearsed, and sure enough, it sent the ultra-logical Centaur-7 way off-script.

"Why," it asked, "is inspiration required in appliance repair?"

One folly breeds another. Before I could master my tongue, I heard myself say, "O, for a muse of fire, to light the brightest Heaven of invention."

Liam glared at me, and no wonder. I've been warned more than once about my tendency to improvise. Don't get me wrong, our entire battalion is proud as a peacock that I can spout other people's chestnuts like there's no tomorrow, but, as Lieutenant Kelsey made abundantly clear back when I first trained for infiltration, free association in the field can get you killed.

Well. No sooner had I let fly with my muse of fire than the Centaur made a clanking, settling noise, and did what no robot ever does: it relaxed. Its head drooped, its shoulders slumped. It didn't quite fall over, but other than that, it looked for all the world like a rag doll lapsing into a coma.

"Liam!" I whispered, completely forgetting to avoid his name. "Look!"

Liam, still nursing his conviction that he should be the one in charge, said, "What the hell did you just do?"

The robot's head tilted up and its equine hindquarters gave a sort of shimmy, as if, in the act of being startled into wakefulness, it was experiencing a muscle spasm. "Hello," it said, in a nuanced, warm, entirely novel voice. "I am Centaur Seven Dash Nine Sixty-Five. How may I be of service?"

There we stood, two badly disguised saboteurs facing down one of the deadliest security bots yet devised, and the damn thing was asking how it could help, as if it were working the front desk of a classy hotel. Assuming this had to be some kind of New Confederation trick, I wanted nothing more than to get my hands on my sidearm, but I'd left it quite intentionally in the toolbox, and the toolbox was in the kitchen. If only I'd had it in hand, I was pretty sure I could squeeze off at least two shots before the Centaur-7 either fired its Taser bolts or flat out gunned me down.

"Say something," Liam whispered.

Not gonna lie, it's hard to be both cowardly and insubordinate all in the same breath, but right there, my partner managed it.

"Centaur-7," I said, unable to remember the rest of its bewildering name, "tell me, what is your function?"

"I am programmed to carry out your commands to the best of my capability."

Liam and I traded a dark *This cannot be happening* look.

"*My* commands," I asked, "in particular?"

"You have spoken a verified Shakespearean quote, so my allegiances have now been redirected to you."

"That's one hell of an override protocol," said Liam.

"Agreed," said the Centaur-7. "It can be inferred that my founding programmer possessed both a sly wit and a wicked sense of ironic humor."

Liam swung around to me. "So, that 'muse' nonsense? That was Shakespeare?"

"Yeah. *Henry V.*"

"Precisely," said the Centaur-7. "All pre-deployment settings are now re-installed."

I said, "Okay, so what if I say something else from Shakespeare? Does that have the reverse effect?"

"Negative, but I am open to additional programming, protocols, and assignments as needed."

This really was the height of insanity. Every active United Alliance battalion spends a good chunk of its mental energy on thinking up ways to evade, trick, or disable Centaur-7 mobile security units, and here we had one ready to do our bidding, lick our hands, and (presumably) use its considerable firepower at our behest—provided, of course, that it was telling the truth.

"All right," I said, facing the robot. "This doorway is way too public. You need to get inside, and, well, I don't know. Do something that seems legit. How about you search the interior of this house? Make certain it's safe."

"Safe from what?" the Centaur-7 asked.

"Terrorists," I replied.

"I will search the premises. I will report back."

The Centaur-7 barely gave us time to clear out of its way as it trotted through the doorway and began its sweep of the house. I'd never seen a Centaur-7 indoors before, and it looked a good deal larger when hemmed in by four clean white walls. Frankly, it also looked ridiculous, nosing around Supply Chief Whitmore's ostentatious, to-the-manor-born stairway as if it were a dog sniffing out trouble.

"Robin," Liam said, as he pulled the door closed behind us, "this could be a major-league opportunity."

That was surely true, but I didn't appreciate his phrasing. Baseball's Major League hadn't operated in at least a decade. During the war, nearly every stadium on both sides had been converted to field hospitals.

Not a pretty end to America's pastime, or my one-time games of catch with my dad.

As the Centaur clopped off to explore the living room, Liam caught my wrist. "I'm not kidding. If we can get this thing home…"

"Home? You want to bring a Centaur-7 back to the nest, maybe over the border?"

"If we can disassemble it, figure out what makes it tick—Robin, this is our chance to learn the damn thing's weaknesses."

I gave him my I'm-in-charge stare. "We just learned its weakness. Shakespeare."

"That can't be system-wide." Then he checked his own logic. "Although, I guess if it isn't system-wide, then the odds of our meeting the exact one we can trigger? Beyond astronomical."

"Trillions to one, sure—unless the whole fleet was set up by one guy, some crank in a lab who didn't like where society was heading and sneaked in a few lines of code to basically say 'Up yours' to the New Confederation."

Looking grim, Liam nodded. "Which is why we have to assume we're being pranked. There is every chance that thing will saunter back into the kitchen, guns blazing, and that'll be that."

I thought this over. The notion that the Centaur had been programmed to trick us was far more plausible than the notion that we'd sprung the lock on a highly whimsical fail-safe, some wacky Easter egg left behind by its original code-master.

"Well," I said, "if its main goal is to kill us, it's had ample opportunity, and if it's trying to lure us into giving up compromising intel, then why is it hiding out in a whole different room?"

Liam shrugged. "No clue."

"Let's get this dishwasher closed back up, so we can get out of here."

"Do you think it'll fit in the van?"

"What, the dishwasher?"

"No! The Centaur."

I lifted my cap, adjusted my idiotic wig, and jammed the cap back on. I had no doubt that the Centaur-7 could fold itself into the back of our service van, but maybe not without ditching half of our tools, not to mention hardware and replacement parts, many of which had taken long months to scrounge.

"Liam," I said, "you deal with the heating element. I'm gonna have a chat with our new friend."

I left Liam in the clutches of the dishwasher and headed off to find the Centaur. Not a difficult task. Centaurs weren't built for stealth, and I could easily hear it tromping around the voluminous living room. When I arrived, it was checking under the throw pillows, searching, presumably, for terrorists. Very small terrorists.

After watching for a moment, I said, "I need to know if you're in cell or sat communication with other Centaur units."

"No," it said, in a dejected tone. "Those links were severed when my protocols were re-set."

"So, you're not in communication with security staff for this compound."

"Negative."

I pressed the point. "Are you sending a passive data stream? Of any sort?"

The Centaur cocked its head in my direction. "I am in active communication with myself, and with you. At the present time, that is all."

"How do I know you aren't lying?"

"My current protocols do not permit the dissemination of falsehoods."

My eyes rolled like the snarky teen I used to be (and not that long ago, either). "How can I trust what you just said?"

The robot considered this for far longer than its processors required. "Without connecting you to one or more of my data ports, I do not see that assertions of truth may be proven. Disinformation is the central problem of the machine condition."

I grinned despite myself. The damned thing sounded downright glum.

Brightening, the Centaur said, "Shall I continue to search for terrorists? Or should we enter into a philosophical debate? I am familiar with the relevant passages in Hume, Aristotle, the Koran, and many others."

"I need to think," I said. "So yes, search, and I'll tag along."

From the kitchen, I heard banging, hammering, and a loud curse, and I resisted an urge to rejoin Liam. Instead, the Centaur and I worked our way into a series of tidy offices, cozy guest bedrooms, and jealousy-inducing bathrooms. It's not like we live so badly back in the nest, but this was luxury of a significantly higher order.

"Okay," I said, "so you're not in communication with any outside systems. What about the house?"

"Supply Chief Whitmore's household AI systems are rudimentary in the extreme."

I frowned. This was a very upscale neighborhood, reserved for military command and ranking civil servants. Tiber Whitmore's home could, through voice command or remote text, do everything that had been promised back in the interactive dawn of the 21st century, and quite a bit more besides. Rudimentary? Well, perhaps it was, to a Centaur-7.

"Hey," I said, "remind me of your name."

"My official designation is too long for most humans to remember. You may call me Dash Nine. What do I call you?"

"Robin."

"Just Robin?"

"If you want titles, I'm Field Ops Corporal Robin Dell."

The robot nodded once, apparently satisfied.

"All right," I said. "Dash Nine, get in touch with the house and locate the safe, if there is one."

"The safe," said Dash Nine, without hesitation, "is in the basement, in the billiards room, behind the liquor cabinet."

"While we're at it, scramble the household video and audio logs for the previous hour, and order it to continue that protocol until we leave."

"Done."

"Great. Now, let's shift our terrorist search to the basement."

It turns out that watching a Centaur-7 clump down a staircase has real entertainment value. Definitely not a picture of grace. However, Dash Nine totally made up for that by instantly extracting the safe's combination from the home security system, and once we were in, I took everything, every last folder, I.D., and data drive. So what if Lieutenant Kelsey had ordered us not to deviate from the basic assignment of installing a single listening device? That train had long since left the station.

As I closed up the safe, being careful not to leave prints, Dash Nine tilted its head toward the ceiling and said, very calmly, "A terrorist has arrived."

I was trying to wrangle my loose armload of intel (the billiards room was kind of shy on bags and boxes). "Where?" I said. "How do you know?"

"'Knowledge makes a king most like his maker.'"

"You want to try that again?"

"The terrorist is in the driveway, now exiting a red pickup truck. I am cognizant of this because I did not interfere with the external feed from the household security cameras."

"And you're still tapped into the system."

"Correct."

I got a better grip on the loose grab-bag of files and said, "Was that more Shakespeare? That knowledge-king quote?"

"Of course. Now, if you'll follow me, I will take us by the most direct route to intercept the terrorist."

Dash Nine didn't wait for a response, and by the time my new best bud reached the front door, I was lagging far behind. Plus, I had to make a quick detour to the kitchen.

"Forget the dishwasher and get these stowed," I said to Liam, who was sitting cross-legged on the floor, parts and tools strewn around him like a tiny bomb blast. Without waiting for an answer, I dumped my armload on the nearest counter and ran for the door.

As I arrived, Dash Nine spun its head one hundred and eighty degrees and said, "The terrorist has stopped approximately three point four six meters from the door. Shall I open up, or open fire?"

"Wait, how do you even know this person's a terrorist?"

"The subject is Latinx, male, and is wearing a New Confederation limitation collar."

Now that was a mouthful. Given the collar, the man on the far side of the door was almost certainly one of those unfortunates who'd gotten caught on the wrong side of the Mexican border when the war broke out, and he hadn't had a green card, or at least not an updated visa, and now he was an indentured servant: fed, housed, and cared for by the benevolent New Confederation. Just to make sure he stayed put and stayed servile, his new masters had kindly outfitted him with one seriously punitive gizmo.

"Dash Nine," I said, "this guy sounds harmless."

"Agreed," said Dash Nine, sounding newly sheepish and even a touch disappointed, "but you instructed me to look for terrorists, and this is the closest we've come so far."

From the kitchen, I heard Liam's plaintive voice asking what was going on. To Dash Nine, I said, "Do not open fire unless I directly order it. Clear?"

"I will not cry havoc, or let loose the dogs of war, unless you insist."

Good enough for me. I hauled open the door.

On the far side stood a heavy-set, weather-beaten man wearing a plaid work shirt, a wide straw hat to keep off the sun, and a pristine limitation collar, pale-blue. In one hand, he held a pair of rust-pocked garden clippers, and when I appeared, he looked up, surprised. Apparently, the primary targets of his nefarious terror plot were the rose bushes on either side of the front walk.

"Oh," I said. "Hi."

The man looked from Dash Nine to me and back again. He slowly raised his hands, presumably thinking he was under arrest. "Whatever I did," he said, his accent light and musical, "I didn't do it."

Ignoring this, I looked along the street, both ways. Liam wasn't actively jamming anything now, and I was kicking myself for so blithely putting myself in view of who knew how many additional cameras and scanner feeds. At least there wasn't any traffic, and no sign of additional Centaur-7s.

Dash Nine leaned close to my ear and spoke in the robot equivalent of a clandestine whisper. "If he is a terrorist, I stand ready to unleash a killing frost."

The man on the doorstep clearly registered this as a lethal threat, and the garden clippers nearly fell from his fingers. "Please, no," he said, and he squeezed his eyes tightly shut.

How had my day veered so far off course? This whole caper had been designed from the ground up to be the most straightforward of missions. Instead? One change-up after another. The safest course would have been to sacrifice this guy for the cause—wrong place, wrong time, an unfortunate casualty of war. But, as Lieutenant Kelsey is fond of pointing out, I've got a stupidly soft heart, and here I stood, facing an enslaved human being, one that I might have the power to help.

Keeping my hat brim low, I said, "*¿Como se llama?*"

"*Me llamo Mateo Orozco. No lo hice, en serio.*"

It occurred to me that he probably couldn't say anything much more controversial than that without setting off the collar. "Okay," I said, "put your hands down. You're here for what, yard work? *¿Las flores?*"

He gestured at the scraggly, unloved roses as if they were the greatest disappointment of his life. *"Las rosas, si. Estan enfermas.* You call it 'black spot.'"

My mother had kept roses before the war, and she'd taught me the basics. No doubt about it, the Whitmore's roses needed help in a big way, but I wasn't sure I cared; the Supply Chief's flower beds didn't qualify as politically neutral.

To Dash Nine, I said, "Is this guy recording us?"

"Confirmed," Dash Nine responded, with a quick nod of its featureless head. "The limitation collar records constantly. It is unlikely, however, that anyone is listening."

"So, it's a passive feed?"

"Approximately five percent of the time, at random, the subject will be observed directly by either human or robot moderators."

I thought about those odds. They seemed pretty great, but not great enough.

Dash Nine inched closer. "Shall I deactivate his communication channels?"

"You can do that?"

"All Centaur-7 units have authorization to access limitation collars."

"Even though we brought you back to your factory settings."

Dash Nine nodded again. "I was disconnected from standard network channels, but all passwords remain functional."

This presented a conundrum. If Dash Nine blocked or switched off the man's collar, that would set off alarms all over the compound. Talk about attracting attention. But if I didn't give that order? If we got out of the compound without trouble, there'd be no reason for anyone to go back and scan through whatever Mateo's collar had already recorded. On the other hand, if pretty much anything went south, I'd already left a virtual ton of compromising data, including the fact that I had somehow tamed a Centaur. Assuming, of course, that I really had.

"Hey, partner!" I called, aiming my voice toward the kitchen, and deliberately avoiding Liam's name. "We need to make tracks!"

He responded with, "On my way!"

I turned back to Mateo. "You got family here?"

Shaking his head, Mateo said, "Here? No. Juarez, and some in El Paso."

La Ciudad Juarez: still under Mexican control. El Paso: still a free city. Either one would be better than here.

To Mateo, I said, "If we get you past New Confederation lines, do you think you could reach El Paso? Would you want to try?"

Mateo's eyes narrowed. I could all but see his racing thoughts. *Should I trust this woman? Or will trusting get me killed?*

Behind me, Dash Nine cleared its non-existent throat. "If we are continuing this conversation, it really might be best to shut down the link-ups to Señor Orozco's collar."

"Once we do that," I said, "we are on the move and making a run for it."

In chatty tones, Dash Nine said, "In case it helps you reach a decision, I must inform you that a fellow Centaur-7 unit is one block away and headed in our direction."

"To this exact address?"

"Network chatter suggests that my signal-silence has attracted attention. This visit represents the first stage of what will become an ever-increasing response. Shall I create a diversion?"

"Um, sure. But how about something not in view of here?"

Sounding downright smug, Dash Nine said, "I must report that the swimming pool pump at 344 Honeysuckle has just experienced an unfortunate and quite spectacular malfunction."

This was the kind of robot I could get sweet on in a hurry. "Liam!" I called. "What's the hold-up?"

"I don't have enough hands!"

Bot-crush or no, it struck me that if Dash Nine were yanking my chain, this was the moment it would turn on us, and as I jogged to the kitchen to help Liam wrangle our gear, I half-expected to feel a sudden spray of bullets. But no. Nothing happened. Liam had our tools ready, and he'd found a sack to stow what I'd dragged from the safe. The dishwasher, with its immaculate stainless steel door closed up, looked peaceful, harmless, but since I hadn't given Liam time to finish, it was probably full of loose parts. No matter. What we had from the safe was intel on a much grander scale—or so I hoped.

At the door, we did a check for overhead drones, found none, and made an orderly retreat to the van. Vans are funny things. There's more room inside than you'd ever believe, and somehow, by bending its torso forward like some long-necked lizard, Dash Nine fit without our having to ditch any inventory. At the very back, Mateo squeezed between Dash Nine's hooves, and in another moment, with me at the wheel, we were on our way.

After two minutes of leisurely driving, we were in sight of the compound's main gate, the same one we'd entered by not an hour before. Liam had his phone out, ready to jam the gatekeeper's feed, but Dash Nine stretched its head forward and said, "'When great leaves fall, the winter is at hand.'"

"Dash," I said, "that's not really helpful."

"What I mean to say," said the robot, "is that the gatekeeper's kiosk is currently occupied by a human."

Liam sat forward, straining to see. "No, it's a bot. It's *always* a bot!"

"The Semblance-4 typically on duty has experienced a temporary electrical malfunction."

I kept driving, and glanced at Liam. "Coincidence?"

"'Coincidences,'" intoned Dash Nine, "'are spiritual puns.'"

Liam and I responded one over top of the other. I said, "What does that even mean?" and Liam, annoyed, said, "That's not Shakespeare."

Sounding affronted, Dash Nine said, "'A foolish consistency is the hobgoblin of little minds.'"

One hand on the wheel, I waved the other in frustration. "That's not Shakespeare, either!"

"In point of fact," said Dash Nine, "I was referencing G.K. Chesterton. Poet, etc. 'Master of paradox.'"

I gave Dash Nine's shoulder a hard shove. "How about you just duck down and keep out of sight?"

"Of course. Operation Duck and Cover, commencing now." Dash Nine retracted itself, and Mateo let out a distant squawk, a reminder that we were tightly packed.

"Everyone stay calm," I said, as I nudged the van over the traffic spikes—no backing out now—and up to the kiosk. Two yards from my front bumper was a simple wooden gate-arm, striped like a candy cane, with a stop sign attached. That wasn't our problem. Three yards beyond that stood a much more substantial gate, eight feet high, black as night, anchored into the compound's wall on both sides, and made of reinforced steel. It reminded me of a coffin lid, seen from the inside.

The kiosk window slid open and a disheveled young woman leaned out, caught in the act of pinning on a name badge. Instead of a standard issue New Confederation jacket, she wore a white button-down like an old-fashioned airline pilot. The patch on her shoulder said "JobTrackers."

I couldn't believe it. To cover for the faulty Semblance-4, the compound had hired a temp.

"Wow!" said the woman. "Beautiful day, huh? I think I'm supposed to see your barcoder?"

I handed it over, and the disc beeped obligingly as she ran the code. All smiles, she said, "Gosh, look at that. It works." Then one of her half-dozen data screens gave her pause. Brow furrowing, she said, "You were at 3644, the Whitmore residence?"

"Yes, ma'am."

"I'm getting a report about a Centaur-7 dispatched to that address that hasn't been responding."

"I'm sure I don't know anything about that."

Next to me, Liam leaned forward, positioning himself to pull a revolver from under the seat. This idiot temp had no idea how close she was to taking a bullet to the head. Another thing she probably didn't know: we were on the clock. Once a barcoder gets scanned, there's a two-minute window to open the compound gate, after which the gate puts itself on lockdown and won't open under any circumstances for a full half hour.

"Bizarre," the woman said, and she rolled a fingertip across the ridgeline of her lower teeth. "Centaur-7s, they don't just...vanish. Do they?"

Lieutenant Kelsey's primary admonition was playing on repeat in my head, *We are not terrorists. We are freedom fighters.*

"Robin," Liam whispered. He was all but begging to end this encounter with a bullet, but before I could decide, Mateo's collar finally figured out he wasn't where he was supposed to be. It let out a chilling rattlesnake hiss and Mateo began screaming as if he were being burned alive.

"Dash!" I yelled, "Shut it down!"

In the same moment, Liam pulled his revolver and did his best to line up a clear shot at the kiosk. As Mateo's collar went silent (well done, Dash), I lunged for Liam's arm, hoping to disrupt his aim.

"Dash!" I cried again, and damned if that robot didn't read my mind. Before Liam could fend me off, Dash dove forward and clamped a single metal hand to Liam's shoulder. I saw (and felt) a flash of blue electricity, and Liam went limp, gulping twice before falling sideways against the glove compartment.

"Don't worry," Dash said, over Mateo's ongoing, rhythmic whimpers. "I will monitor your partner's cardiac activity. I will also monitor Mateo, the gardener who is not a terrorist. You deal with the gate."

"You can't open it?"

"Negative. The compound gate is disconnected from all network feeds. You have to press the button."

I turned my attention to the kiosk, where the cowering temp was staring right at me, too terrified to look away. Because the kiosk was set (by design, I'm sure) too close to the pavement, I couldn't open the driver's side door, which left me with one option and one only: the truth.

"Listen," I said, "here's the deal. We're the terrorists you've heard so much about. United Alliance, in the flesh. The enemy. But we've got family and friends, just like you, and right now, you've got about thirty seconds to open that gate before it triggers an alarm, and if that alarm goes off, everyone in this van dies, and so will you, because New Confederation intelligence services will have every reason to question you, and even if they don't kill you in the process, you'll wish they had. But, if my friends and I roll out of here peacefully, no one will have any reason to question you about anything. So, I am begging you. It's a win-win if you press that button."

In a sandpaper whisper, the woman said, "I should call security."

"Fifteen seconds," I said.

I couldn't see her hands, but her left arm reached toward her control panel.

"Come on," I said, exhorting her. "Screw your courage to the sticking-place."

She blinked, surprised. "I remember that. We read it in school. *MacBeth*."

"Ten seconds," I said. It was only an estimate, but I needed a prod—and it worked. Her arm shifted, angling toward a different button. She pressed it. The gate groaned with the effort and notched upward; a strip of daylight rose along its base, as bright white as a sunlit snow-scape.

Do people truly breathe sighs of relief? I know I did.

The temp rubbed a hand over her mouth and said, as I shifted the van into drive, "Let me come with you."

"You jump ship, they'll be on our tail in seconds."

"I could help. I could fight!"

The wooden gate swung upwards as its huge metal counterpart reached its full height and clanked to a stop. We had a free shot to the highway.

"You want to fight?" I said. "Then stay here, and don't give us away."

"But I want to come with you!"

She looked ready to shimmy through the kiosk window, and from there into the van. If she tried, I'd have to push her back, maybe even shoot her—which gave me an idea.

"Dash," I said, "can you lean forward enough to take her picture?"

An extension rod like an old antenna snaked out of Dash's shoulder, narrowly missing my head. "Done," Dash said. "Also, the gate will close in twelve seconds."

I turned back to the temp. "What's your name?"

Eyes welling, sniffling, she said, "Kayla."

"Okay, listen. Kayla. We've got your photo, which means we can track you. And on another day, with planning, we can run you to our side of the border. But it can't be now."

I hit the gas without waiting for a reply; covert wars just don't have time for the poetry of fare-thee-well. In another moment, we were past the gate and gone, mission accomplished.

Sort of.

In short order, we'd rendezvous with our pit crew, switch vehicles, and be back at the nest in time for lunch. Mateo would be sent to tactical, where they'd work on removing his collar. Liam would head to the infirmary, leaving me to face down a nasty debriefing. I figured the odds were high that I'd get tossed out of field work for good, but frankly, I was pretty sure I deserved a medal. I mean, who

else ever brought home a working (and downright friendly) Centaur-7?

"Hey, Dash," I said, as the compound faded in the rear-view mirror, "how's Liam?"

"Vitals are normal, but I doubt he'll wake any time soon."

I nodded. It occurred to me that Liam might be trouble, in future. It was entirely possible I'd made myself a long-term enemy. If that were the case, it would be doubly unfortunate, since in the long years before I got promoted to Field Ops Corporal, Liam and I had been friends.

To Dash Nine, I said, "You know, when we get back, some of the lab techs are gonna want to take you apart."

Dash Nine shifted restlessly. "You will not let them."

"Buddy, the day someone cuts into you, it's over my dead body."

Machines don't laugh, but Dash Nine managed a pretty good approximation. Then it said, "Are you familiar with *Casablanca*?"

"Say what?"

My hulking killer robot laughed again. "Robin, I do believe this is the start of a beautiful friendship."

My derision came out as a snort. "Either that, or this is a seriously complicated ruse to get me to drive you back to the nest. And once there, you lay waste to everyone in sight."

For a long moment, Dash Nine said nothing.

"Dash," I said, "tell me that's not what's happening here."

One of the Centaur-7's better processors let out a wonderfully human sigh. "Is it possible," said Dash Nine, "that I understand friendship better than you?"

Mark Rigney has had over fifty short pieces find print in a gentle arc covering the last two decades, with stories in Lightspeed, Realms of Fantasy, and more. Theatrical credits, too, with play across the U.S., including off-Broadway, along with Canada, Hong Kong, Nepal, and Australia.

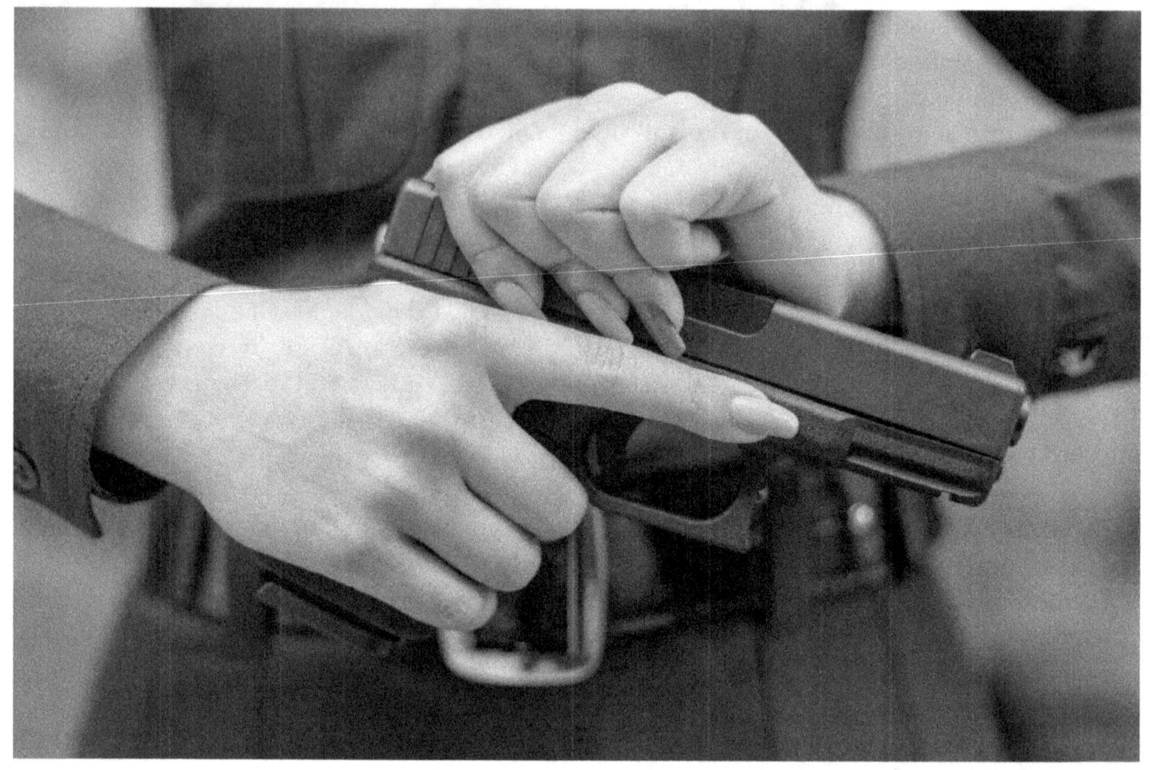

Extraordinary Lessons for Startling Success
Carol Gore

This is the story an ordinary girl, born with nothing but determination, equipped with only her wits, who, against all odds, arose to triumphant peaks so high it would make most people dizzy. Are you thinking, there's no way *I* could do that? Well, the bad news is, you can't. Not with that mindset! Relinquish all doubt. Trust in your own potential. Read on, and I will reveal the extraordinary lessons that led to my startling success.

We begin in the year 2117, when I first arrived at the big, shimmering city of Holdings, Colobraska. You can only imagine how a girl of eighteen years, fresh from the Floodplains, felt when she stepped off the nuke train for the first time, and beheld skyscrapers such as she had never seen in all her life. I remember it well. It was fire season, and the smog clouds were lit a soft orange like that of the most beautiful sunset. I took a deep breath of the city air and coughed. So different it was from the amphibious landscape I was used to! The air was thick with smoke, not humidity. It smelled of cozy campfires, not seaweed and rotten sewage. There would be a lot to get used to here.

A strong male voice sounded over the loudspeakers, and my fellow passengers and future interns fell in line and shuffled towards the nearest exit. We were all in the same situation. Our parents had traded our labor for rations of bread. We came from all over—the Floodplains, Tinder Woods, the Texahoma Desert. During our journey, I'd been forced to endure the grousing of my peers. They blamed their parents for selling them to a company they deemed "evil" and equated our internship to slavery. I kept silent amidst these complainers. I saw it as a win-win for my parents and myself. The twice monthly shipments of bread would supplement their diets of snails and kelp.

And I would embark on a path of possibility and opportunity. That is the first lesson I must impart to you: always keep a positive attitude!

We were loaded into a succession of vans that would carry us to our destiny. Of course, my traveling companions continued their grumblings. The worst was a boy, tall, with sun-bleached hair and deeply tanned skin, features that telegraphed he was from the desert. A few teens surrounded him, listening with soft eyes and parted lips while he proudly proclaimed that he wouldn't be the property of Daily Bread, not for long, at least.

I distracted myself from this negativity by watching the bustling city life from the van window. The happy city-dwellers strolled down sidewalks covered by thick domed glass amongst verdant trees, bushes, and cheerful blossoms. Squinting through the dusty orange haze, I promised myself I would one day walk among them. Our contract stated we'd serve as interns in perpetuity. Yet, there were rumors of worthy interns being promoted to the corporate office on recommendation by their superiors. Though rare, and derided by many as entirely false, I held fast to this hope, which brings me to my next lesson: strike the word 'impossible' from your vocabulary!

The vans deposited us at an enclave of warehouses on the outskirts of the city. After we were showered, deloused, and given the Daily Bread branding, we were shown to our new home where we would eat, sleep, and work. Bunkbeds lined the perimeter of the vast building. In the center, stacked in clear boxes, lived our squirming charges—the small, yet mighty, mealworms.

After a weeklong training period, we fell into our routine. The days were busy, filled with tasks to keep our mealworms clean and fed until we harvested the happy things to be dried and ground into the flour for the world's daily bread. Our eyes adjusted to the low light, and our bodies to the steady 85 degree heat—essentially, we humans enjoyed the same habitat that sustained our mealworms. We ate the same food too, a dried grain mix topped with a little water to soften it. And, delightfully, the mealworms were also nourished by a substance we made with our own bodies, colloquially known as night soil. When it was time to knock off, we'd collapse into our bunks, exhausted, yet proud in the fact that we'd put in a hard day's work.

Well, some of us. The desert boy I mentioned before, who's name I soon learned was Harvey, occupied the bunk next to mine. He'd whisper into the night, and through a game of telephone, what he said spread through the warehouse. Apparently, this fellow was a revisionist history enthusiast. I'd squeeze the pillow against my ears while he lectured on the Constitution, that dusty bit of parchment that hadn't been relevant in decades. He claimed that if the Constitution was still in effect, not one of us would be living in these conditions, working without pay or any choice in the matter. I'd often find myself shaking in bed, wanting to shout that we weren't working without pay! We were given a place to sleep, food to eat, and our families were rewarded handsomely for our sacrifice! This Constitution he touted had done little more than quell industry, the industry, I'd add, that provided you your daily bread and that was why they'd scrapped the wretched thing!

It is with regret that I must admit I didn't shout these words. I swallowed them whole and let them fester in my stomach while allowing him to pontificate unchallenged. Why my silence? I'm not sure. Perhaps I was a bit shy. Mostly, I felt it wouldn't do any good. You see, there are two kinds of people in this world; the kind like Harvey who gripe and complain, and my kind, who do their work quickly, efficiently, and with a smile, knowing that if you wish to better your situation, you simply have to work your way out of it.

After many months of dedication (Do you sense a lesson here? Patience, dear pupil!), my efforts did not go unnoticed. Seath, one of our den fathers, took a liking to me. Oh, he didn't lavish me with praise, pat me on the head, or declare me a "good girl." But never once, during all my tenure, did he assign me to clean the night soil collection system. On those special days when we were afforded vegetables, or meat after a faithful intern had completed their contract, he made sure I was served first and of the choicest bits. If I reported bed bugs in my bunk, I needed only wait a few days— a week at most— for the situation to be remedied.

Of course, the path to success is often a lonely one. The special treatment I'd earned caused my fellow interns to suffer intense bouts of jealousy. When I wasn't being shunned, I was spat upon, tripped, and once locked in the night soil chamber while depositing my donation. I wish I could say this didn't bother me. Though I longed for success above all else, I was also very lonely. I missed my home. At night, I dreamt of wet sand squishing between my toes, the nomadic nature of islands as they popped up randomly only to be flooded again, salt on my tongue and in my hair.

Sometimes I'd hold a mealworm in my palm, fantasizing that this little creature would be sent to my parents in the form of bread, and that my efforts were directly nourishing their bodies. "Tell them I wish them well," I'd whisper.

There were days when I felt my efforts were getting me nowhere, when even Seath's subtle displays of support weren't enough. Those days were long and dark. I worked harder, faster, never complained, and yet I couldn't see the light at the end of the tunnel. When would I rise from this warehouse? When would I truly be valued? Was I destined to complete my contract, my body reused as nourishment for a fresh round of interns?

I was in a vulnerable state such as this when Harvey approached me. Though we'd been working together for close to a year, we'd yet to speak directly to each other. I was replenishing the substrate for the mealworms, and placing sliced potatoes on top.

"Seems like they eat better than us," he said, sidling up to me.

"Sorry?" I looked at him in confusion, not sure if he was actually talking to me. Just behind him, a cluster of interns pretended to work, but their ears were cocked in our direction. He repeated himself, though I'd heard him quite clearly the first time. I responded with little more than a shrug and went back to my task.

He raked a hand through his shaggy hair, which had regained a darker pigment due to his lack of sun. I'll admit, reader, he was an attractive sort, and I certainly felt a pull in his direction. I was so flustered, I dropped a bit of potato. He retrieved it for me and placed it in my hand. His skin was warm and set my heart to racing. I'm sure my emotions were displayed all over my face, because Harvey gave a self-satisfied smirk.

"You don't participate in our meetings," he said in a low voice.

Meetings. It was such a simple word, but I felt the danger dripping off of it. I scanned the warehouse for Seath. I couldn't risk him witnessing this subversive conversation.

"You could hear something that might interest you," Harvey continued.

I turned to him, which was odd for me because I never diverted attention from my work. "I can hear you talking loud and clear while I'm trying to sleep. And it doesn't interest me in the least."

At that, he got rather angry. He kept his volume low, though the tension was there. He told me I shouldn't work so hard. That I was throwing the quotas off and making it more difficult for the rest of them. He called me a cog in the machine. A bootlicker. And on and on. I withstood this abuse until he finally tired and walked off in a huff. The group of interns listening in practically stabbed me with their icy glares, but it was nothing I wasn't used to.

I tried to brush off Harvey's rudeness, but for the next few days I lived in a state of roiling anger. How dare he speak to me like that? If my work ethic was making their lives so miserable, why didn't they work harder? Regrettably, this distraction caused me to make quite a few mistakes and my productivity suffered.

Seath noticed. The day he called me into his office to discuss my sudden lackluster performance, I had the most horrible pain in the pit of my stomach. I stood before his desk while he reviewed my productivity report. I kept seeing Harvey's face—so attractive, so smug. This was all his fault.

Seath finished reading, leaned back in his chair, tapping the desk with his baton. "What's happening here?"

I was prepared to apologize, to take whatever punishment I deserved and promise to do better. But then inspiration hit. Why not tell the truth? Why roll over and be blamed for Harvey's trouble-making? And why hadn't I thought of this before?

So I laid it all bare. Speaking in a calm, measured voice, I detailed the nightly meetings on the Constitution, individual and workers' rights, democracy. I explained how Harvey had tried to lure me in, and subsequently led to the decline of my productivity. I speculated that his talks caused the other interns to work less out of spiteful pride. Seath listened carefully, showing no reaction. When I finished, the corner of his mouth twitched.

"Thank you for telling me," he said.

Silence stretched for a long space of time.

"What about my punishment?"

He waved me away.

I left his office, heart lifted. This is perhaps one of the most important lessons I can give you: any obstacle can be turned to your advantage.

That very night, while Harvey was in the middle of his nauseating soliloquy, the warehouse doors flew open, followed by the rhythmic stomping of a half dozen men. Clad in all black and armed with machine guns, the small militia marched straight to Harvey and yanked him to his feet. His devout disciples screamed, cursed, and spat at the men. They grabbed Harvey's feet and clothing to stop him from being dragged away. They were rewarded for their devoted frenzy with swift kicks to the kneecaps by (judging from the crunching sound) steel-toed boots. One girl would not release her arms from around his waist until her nose met brutally with the butt of a gun.

Harvey finally put an end to this nonsense by announcing, "Stop. I will return."

The men silently led him out of the warehouse. When the doors slammed shut, those who'd fought for him wailed and sobbed, keeping up this racket throughout the night.

The first few days following Harvey's departure, it seemed I was the only one who remembered how to work. Seath quickly regained control. After a few public beatings and withholding of rations, conditions changed immensely and for the better. My fellow interns shuffled through their tasks like dutiful robots, too dejected to even play their cruel pranks on me. Though none were as efficient as I, our overall productivity steadily increased. Harvey was the bad seed after all, and thanks to me, had been rooted out so we could flourish and thrive.

I was proud of my accomplishment, but also a bit depressed. I'd gone above and beyond, proven myself not only as hardworking, but also unshakably loyal. What had it gotten me other than more of the same? In moments of weakness, some of Harvey's past words resonated in my heart. Perhaps Daily Bread *was* evil and cared nothing for us beyond exploiting our labor. Perhaps corporations such as Daily Bread and others *had* destroyed society, trashed the environment, and eroded our freedoms all in the name of profit.

I shook these silly notions away, until the straw came to break the proverbial camel's back. The night soil collection system clogged and overflowed. Seath obliviously stepped in the brown, stinking puddle. He hiked his pants up instinctively, and I caught a glimpse of the Daily Bread branding on his right ankle. I was positively livid! The rumors were true, and Seath had been promoted from the internship. Even though I'd impressed him, he'd offered no helping hand.

One morning, instead of being promptly shuffled to work after breakfast, the den fathers set up a projection screen. We were told we were being given a treat. Naively, my heart went all a flutter. I thought I was getting my due. Seath had prepared a film presentation chronicling my achievements, and I was to be promoted in a rousing ceremony. The lights fell. The film started. And I felt I'd been slapped in the face with a wet rag.

It was the same film we were shown at our orientation, a Daily Bread produced feature that chronicled the corporation's rise. There were old reels of the famines, dusty farms in the west, my beloved Floodplains in the east. Refugees arrived by the busload to the middle of the country. People starved and suffered until the innovative thinkers that founded Daily Bread Inc began raising mealworms, crickets, and roaches for human consumption.

During the viewing, there was a kerfuffle at the entrance. The doors opened and we all shielded our eyes from the sun. Out of that burst of light appeared Harvey. He was barely recognizable. His limbs were spindly, his hair thin, the left side of his face swollen and bruised. He leaned heavily on two guards that assisted him. The interns gasped. Some cried. A few hid their faces. Harvey was placed unceremoniously on a bench positioned right next to the screen, his wrists and ankles shackled. He remained motionless

as the film played out, his head hanging nearly to his lap.

Afterwards, a few interns tried to approach him. Seath promptly struck them with a baton. Harvey remained chained in his seat throughout the day, and into the evening after the lights were cut. The next day, I was assigned to his care, instructed to give him an ounce of water every three hours. Seath explained that I was the only person for the job, since I was immune to his dangerous ideas. I gave him my usual perky nod, expertly masking the burning resentment I felt inside.

The first few times I brought Harvey his water, he ignored me. He didn't even lift his head or acknowledge my presence. Then, he took to swatting the water away, weakly whispering, "fuck you," under his breath.

Once, in the dead of night, I approached him with my cup. Security had tightened since his detainment. Instead of a sleeping guard posted at each of the two entrances, there were now ten, prowling the warehouse as we slept, machine guns hanging at their sides. When Harvey made to knock the cup from my hand, I grabbed his thin wrist.

"Do you mean to die here?" I said. "To let them kill you?"

Mustering all of his strength, he raised his head. His face was dry, the skin flaking around his eyes and lips. "You did this."

I dropped to my knees, grasping his brittle hand. "I am with you," I whispered, then kissed his scaled knuckles.

He kept his eyes on me as I lifted the cup to his lips. He drank greedily.

From then on, he allowed me to care for him. Often, I brought three ounces of water instead of the prescribed one. When I could, I mixed dried grains into his cup, or slipped him a sliced potato meant for the mealworms. He gradually regained strength, and the fire relit in his eyes. He'd give me snippets of messages and instructions to be passed around the warehouse. I'd relay these to the interns around the night soil collection chamber, in the menstruation tent, whenever and where ever I could. His teachings spread faster than the stomach viruses that plagued us. Eventually, we had a plan.

Reader, before you judge me as a turncoat, please recognize the lesson here: be willing to shift allegiances when it suits your needs.

The appointed night arrived. Everyone knew their roles and were eager to act. Tension crackled in the air as we waited in our beds. At precisely one am, a female intern began to convulse and issue distorted screams. "She's having a seizure!" her neighbor declared. When a guard approached, this same neighbor thrust a handful of night soil into the man's mouth. He gave a frenzied reaction, gasping and spitting and dropping to his knees. Another intern obtained the machine gun, and promptly put the poor night soil covered man out of his misery.

Naturally, chaos ensued. The other guards grouped together and responded, the rat-a-tat-tat of their bullets echoing through the cavernous walls. They slaughtered the girl who'd started it all, her neighbor with the night soil, and a few more. This counter attack was short lived. A group of forty interns banded together, and overwhelmed the guards by piling on top of them. I watched the writhing pile of limbs and the occasional explosion of bullets and blood, stunned that my colleagues would lay down their lives instead of simply working harder to better their situation, but I digress.

There were close to two hundred of us and ten of them, so with some bloodshed, we were able to overtake them and apprehend the weapons. In the confusion, all the guards were executed. Harvey was quite perturbed at this, as he'd counted on holding them hostage to leverage his list of demands. While the interns celebrated — cheering, turning over the bunks, arranging the guards' bodies in comical positions — Harvey pulled a group of four, including me, aside to discuss the problem. I suggested we wait for Seath and

the other den fathers to arrive for their shift and use them as hostages. Harvey gave me a smile that showed he was impressed, which in turn sent a shiver straight down to my toes. The lesson here is: always be ready to think on your feet.

We had a few hours yet to wait. I prepared the grain mix and encouraged everyone to eat, which was no easy task in their excited state. They drank it down quickly and with no enjoyment. Harvey regaled us with the demands. Whoever wanted to leave would be free to do so. Whoever remained would be paid adequately and receive better lodging. There would be healthcare and days off and on and on. He presented a glorious utopia, to be sure, yet I harbored doubts that corporate would yield to such.

Seath and the other den fathers arrived at eight am sharp, as usual. We were ready. As soon as they entered the warehouse, we were on them. Held at gunpoint, they surrendered their weapons, and allowed themselves to be tied to chairs in Seath's office. I volunteered to guard them, saying heroically to Harvey, "Leave them to me." I was issued a machine gun, and barricaded myself in with them.

Seath watched me, silent except for the grinding of his teeth. Finally, he said, "Just what are you trying to accomplish?"

I told him Harvey's brilliant plan, and assured him he would be freed as soon as our demands were met. Seath sneered. "That won't work. Corporate doesn't give a shit about us. They'll drop a bomb on this place before they negotiate with you."

I shrugged. "I know."

I allowed the silence to stretch between us, giving space for Seath's thoughts to go where I wanted them to go. When it felt right, I said, "I can stop this right now."

He didn't seem to believe me. Still, he said, "Then you'd better stop it. Or we'll all fucking die."

"What does that matter to me? I'm just an intern, stuck here in perpetuity. Death would be better than this." I sighed, pretending to be quite forlorn. "Unless, you promise to recommend me for a promotion. Then I'd have something to live for."

"Interns don't get promoted."

"Is that right?" Using the end of the gun, I lifted his pant leg, revealing his old branding. Well, the look on his face was simply priceless, a mixture of shock and shame that dissolved into resignation. I leveled my gaze at him, letting it go without saying that things could've been much simpler if he'd recommended me for promotion earlier.

Seath agreed to these terms, then was thrown off balance when I simply relaxed in the chair, legs crossed. "What are you going to do?"

"It's already been done. You see, Seath, I had faith in you."

Harvey and the others were still finalizing the demands when the night soil I'd slipped into the grain mixture began its work on their systems. The effect was like dominoes falling. The line to the donation chamber wound around the warehouse. They dragged mattresses off of the overturned bunks and lay there, clutching their cramping stomachs. I pretended to nurse them, and in their weakened state, managed to quietly gather all the weapons, which I brought, one by one, to the office.

After I untied him, Seath did his part by calling in a militia. Harvey was crouched in a corner, dehydrated and shaking when they stormed in. He was thrown off guard at first, but as the men began marching around restoring order, he grit his teeth, the muscles in his jaw twitching. His eyes found me quickly. I tried to speak to him telepathically, to get across that I hated it had to end this way, that though his ideas sounded really nice they were just too far-fetched, and that I was just like him, trying to get ahead, the difference being, perhaps, that I was more realistic. I don't think Harvey got all that. He scrunched his face up as if he might cry, then hung his head in defeat. That was the last I ever saw of him.

This is the final lesson I will gift to you, and one I want you to hold close to your heart: you have to put yourself first. Fight with the masses, and you will die with the masses. Fight for yourself, and you will rise above them all.

Seath was called to the main office to give a full report. When the car arrived to take him there, I got in with him without asking for permission. He upheld his part of the bargain and told the company all I'd done to stop the uprising, and recommended me for promotion. They created a new position for me. As a "source," I'd work in another warehouse looking for signs of insurrection and report them immediately. I served this role for three years, hopping from warehouse to warehouse. Then I trained sources for two years. Finally, I obtained a cubicle in the corporate office where I oversaw the training of the source trainers.

Since then, I have lived a charmed life indeed. I've walked the lush city sidewalks, enjoyed lunches at outdoor cafes, chatted with co-workers in the break room, lived in my own apartment, and so much more. Tomorrow, my story ends. You see, reader, I have reached the pinnacle of success. My salary is so high that Daily Bread can no longer afford me. I'll be the first female granted the honor of entering the retirement chamber, where I'll be gently coaxed to sleep, never to awake again. What will I dream during this deep slumber? I cannot imagine, as all of my dreams in life have been realized.

Carol Gore examines the absurdity of life on earth by writing humor and speculative fiction, sometimes at the same time. She received an MFA from the California College of the Arts in San Francisco. She's the author of the 80's horror inspired novella, INFESTED, and her fiction has appeared in Dark Moon Digest, Fourteen Hills, All Worlds Wayfarer, and others. She lives in the rural south with her husband and two sons.

The Road to Shambala
Naomi Vondell

"You're keeping a human as a pet?"

My question is simple. So is my gut-wrenching, visceral reaction to the white mass of jiggling flesh I see in the stall in front of me.

"He's a rescue."

Pel and I stand and look at the naked human. I've never seen anything so disgusting in my life. Blubbery, mottled skin with hairs growing out of moles. A bushy white beard on its face. Clearly old and male, the human shuffles around in its stall, looking vaguely around with its two stupidly blinking eyes. It grunts and snorts, and then finally sits down on the bench.

"Where did you get him?"

"You remember that night I couldn't hang out with you? I, uh, sort of went on a raid."

I look straight at Pel. "A raid? On what?"

"Atrok Labs."

"Pel...you could get in trouble."

"I know."

"They have security all over the place."

"I don't care."

With effort, I look back at the human, who's now peeing in a corner. *The most disgusting thing about them. Shooting that smelly liquid out of their bodies.* "Have you given it a name?"

"'Him'. Not 'it'." Pel's voice sounds distant. "Snuffy."

"Snuffy? Oh, I get it! Because he has a nose. Cute."

"I'm glad you think so." Pel shuffles a couple of his feet. "Are we still dating?"

"Of course." I smile at him. "But I might have to connect with you on MindNet only for the foreseeable future."

"Okay, lovebug." He kisses me. "Now, how about we study for tomorrow's test?"

I walk home from Pel's place the long way. I never particularly want to face my parents. They will never fully understand me.

I can feel the spring sun beating down upon me as I make my way down the cobblestone sidewalk. Through the nostril-holes in my shirt, I breathe in the wholesome air. Over the olfactory sensors on my arms wafts the heady scent of lilac.

My head is filled with thoughts of my boyfriend. He's a little odd, for sure. A pet human? Humans are easily the most disgusting species on this planet. Not only do the vile little critters live in the ground, but they run around filthy and naked, with their nasty parts flopping around for the world to see. They drop their poop everywhere and have litters right in the streets. I prefer them on my dinner plate where they belong.

Suddenly I hear a high-pitched yell behind me. A cluster of feral humans, probably a litter of cubs, jumps out from a hole in the ground. The biggest one begins to chase me, screaming gibberish. The mom protecting her young.

I jump out of the way and start running. I step in a puddle of yellow liquid. *Oh, great. Now I'm going to smell like pee.*

I look behind me. The ferals seem to have lost interest, and the mom's feeding the cubs. Breathing a sigh of relief, I shudder in horror and continue on my way home.

The smell of the barbecue makes my arms and legs tingle with anticipation.

I walk into the backyard and crouch into the nearest hammock. Dad, holding a drink in his upper right hand, waves his upper left hand at me while his lower left motions me over to the lounging area. The meaty aroma wafts through the yard. I feel a little guilty, but I love it.

"Tough day at school, Roka?"

"We have a calculus test tomorrow."

"That's circles, right?"

"Curves, Dad." I try not to roll *all* my eyes.

"Oh. Well, I'm sure you'll do well. You've always had a head for numbers." He takes a thoughtful sip of his blood martini and stirs the ice around. "Where's your brother?"

"Probably in his room playing games on MindNet. Go easy on that stuff, Dad."

"I'm okay. Just an aperitif."

"'Aperitif' nothing."

My mom walks over to us with a large plate of steaming-hot burgers. "Here," she says to Dad. "Better get some food into you."

"Matti, I'm fine. I worked all day and then took care of the kids. Can't I enjoy a little refreshment before dinner?"

"It's every night, Jool. You have a problem." She flips a burger onto his plate. "Eat this before you say more words."

"Sexist."

I sigh. "Mom, can't you two give it a rest for one night?"

Mom manages something close to a smile. "Certainly." A few of her eyes blink. "How was school today?"

"Good."

"'Good.' That's informative. Come on, Roka. Talk to us."

As she pours me a drink of lime soda from the pitcher on the table, I sigh. *The older generation will never understand me. May as well rattle off some kind of description to shut her up.*

"I logged in first thing in the morning. Mrs. Boosh was late, but most of my study group was there and we got a head start. First class was History of Arachnean Evolution, so we learned all about millions of years ago when we all used to crawl around in dirt and build webs in trees."

"Oh, that's nice." My dad smiles his weak smile and takes another drink.

"By the way, you wouldn't have survived back in the old days, Dad. Mom would've swallowed you whole by now."

I let that sink in. Mom bristles. "We're not spiders, dear. We're Arachneans. Although you wouldn't know that by looking at your room."

"I'll clean it up." I won't. Even if I do say it every night. *Anyway, isn't tomorrow the day the cleaning gentleman comes?*

Mom leans forward. "Did I overhear that you have a calculus test?"

"Yeah." *This is going to lead to something. I know it.*

"Have you studied for it?"

"Pel and I just did. Over at his place after school."

"Pel? *Sturma* Pel?"

"Yep." I keep my eyes on the cobblestone patio and wait for the other shoes to drop.

"Of the South Side Sturmas?"

"Yep."

My mom lowers her voice. "I'm a little concerned about you associating with that boy. Do you even know anything about him?"

"I know he's kind, and he really cares about me." *And he never nags me,* I want to add.

She sucks on her burger. "What kind of work does his mother do?"

"Actually, his mother stays at home. His father works."

"What?" My dad nearly chokes on his drink. "They've got that backward, don't they?"

My mother's voice goes deadly quiet. "Well, what kind of work does his *father* do, then?"

"He's an electrician."

"Oh. A skilled trade." She stares straight ahead.

"I guess they're a *progressive* family, then?" My father has never liked the word.

"I guess so." I take my drink over to the bar and spritz it with a shot of vodka.

"What're this boy's…opinions like?" My mother shoots a disapproving glance at the drink in my hand.

"I don't know." I'm lying, and I'm sure it shows because I can feel my right central eye tic kicking in. "He's kind to everyone. All the kids like him. He gets straight A's in class. He helped me study for the calculus test."

"Yeah, yeah, I'm sure he understands circles and stuff like that. I meant what are his views?"

"Well, I'm assuming he thinks men should pursue higher education and careers? I don't know." *And he has a pet human…*

"How does his father balance his career with his responsibilities toward his family?"

"I don't like it." My dad is sipping rhythmically now. "One of those hippie kids. You never know what kind of smut they're peddling."

"Dad, Pel doesn't 'peddle' anything. He helps me with calculus."

"Just be careful." My mom leans forward and focuses all her eyes on me. "We don't want you to get hurt."

"Whatever." I take a long sip of my spiked soda, place it on the table with an audible click, and force a smile.

My mother breaks the ensuing silence with a clap of her two upper arms. "Want a burger?"

"Sure."

"The finest brisket cut." She hands me a plate and flips a burger onto it. "Mustard, ketchup, relish?"

"No thanks. Straight up."

"You got it."

Brisket, I think as I suck in its juices. *Hopefully from the chest of a human that didn't eat too much fat.* For just a moment, as I bite into my burger, I imagine what Pel would think of me. Then I put him out of my mind.

As I enjoy my mother's delicious meal, I inwardly smile. I know something they don't know.

I'm looking forward to tonight.

I sit at my desk and carefully fit the helmet over my head. The magnetic chinstrap snaps into place. I concentrate as the electrodes on the helmets make contact.

Normally, I'd go wireless. But I can't risk snooping parents. I pick up my glass, still filled with vodka and soda, from the desk. I wince as the smell of leftover food from the food liquefier on my desk wafts over my arms.

I close my eyes.

"Hey." Pel's voice in my head is deep and sonorous. His face looms in my mind.

"Hey, beautiful," I say back.

"Charmer. How do you think you'll do on the test?"

"Just okay. I'm not a mathlete like you."

"I don't know if I'm a mathlete. I think I'm more of an artistic type."

"You can be a mathlete and still be masculine."

"Tough to do." He laughed. "Want to take a walk?"

"Okay."

Suddenly we're in a moonlit field, walking in tall grass. Crickets chirping. Distant trees waving in the wind.

"This is so nice." I take a deep breath of fresh air, and my arms sense the slight aroma of clover. "Where is it?"

"Ireland."

"Where?"

He smiles. "It's an ancient name for the western part of Isok."

We hunch in silence, staring up. Pel motions to a swirl of stars in a curved line. "See that? The Palm Tree."

"It's beautiful." I look at him and just breathe.

"It's said the ancient Arachneans used to hide from prehistoric humans in that tree. Then it flew into the sky so we could be safe forever in love and peace."

"So," I muse, "we're in an ancient land. Should we expect a horde of humungous humans any time soon?"

"There might be some. But they were mostly shy. They won't bother us if we don't bother them."

"Well, if we do meet any, I'll protect you."

"I feel so safe with you." He shoots me a wry smile. "No, really: they're more afraid of us than we are of them."

"I doubt it." I shudder. "Humans are gross. They're so *slimy*. All that wet stuff on their skin. Dead skin cells trailing off everywhere. And then there's that *thing* in the middle of their faces."

"Yeah, their noses. It's how they smell."

"You see? Why can't they smell with their arms and legs like everybody else?"

"They breathe through it too."

"Yeah, well, they must have air whooshing through their brains! Why can't they have nostrils in their bellies like normal?" I shoot him a sideways glance. "Yours are sexy."

Pel throws his head back and laughs. I notice his soft, sensitive neck. "You really know how to seduce a guy."

"Sorry." I reach out my upper right arm and caress his dark, shiny neck. My three fingers follow the curve from his neck to his back. With my upper left arm, I gently stroke his black hair and cup his cheek. "Wanna make out?"

"Yeah."

We link all our arms together and settle into an embrace.

Suddenly he pulls back. "Roka…have you told your parents about us?"

"Sort of."

"What does that mean, exactly?"

I look down. "They know we study together. They know you helped me with tomorrow's test."

He sighs. "Roka, if we're going to be together, it has to be out in the open. I don't sneak around."

"I know, I know. You have to understand about my parents. They're very conservative. They wouldn't *get* you."

"I don't know about that. I'm great with parents." He raises three of his eyebrows. "Don't you think it's time we all met?"

"I – I guess so." I swallow. "Why don't you come over for dinner tomorrow?"

"I'm there."

"It's barbecued rump steak. Out on our patio. Just thought you should be prepared."

"Oh, don't worry." He gives me a quadruple wink with all four of his left eyes. "I will be."

"Let me pour you a drink." My father can always be depended on to try to diffuse the tension with alcohol.

"Haven't you had enough, Dad?"

"You know I always have a drink or three before dinner. We're about to chow down on prime cap. In fact, I think your mother's almost ready to serve them up."

Pel shifts in his hammock. "I'm fine, thanks. I'm not old enough to drink anyway."

"Oh, come on, live a little. How do you like your steak?"

Pel casts a side-eye glance at the grill. His throat pulsates ever so slightly.

"No steak for me, thanks. I brought my own portabella mushrooms for the grill."

My dad blinks. "Why?"

"I'm a vegan."

My dad slowly puts down his martini. I can feel my heart sinking into my stomach.

"You're a what?"

"A vegan."

"What does that mean?"

"I don't eat meat." He looks at my mom as if she's about to serve him a plate of virus. Then he looks at me as if I'm about to eat it.

"None at all?"

"None at all."

"Why not?"

"I believe meat is inherently cruel."

Dad takes a swig of his martini. "What do you mean? What does it do to you? Upset your stomach?" I groan inwardly. *What a dad joke.*

"No, I don't mean meat is cruel to me. I mean it's cruel of Arachneans to harvest and kill humans for their body parts."

I jump in. "He also doesn't wear leather or use hairspray tested on humans." I know I'm speaking with rapid nervousness.

Dad raises an arm to me to silence me and stares at Pel with all eyes fixed. "So you're like one of those long-haired young folks holding signs outside the meatpackers?"

Pel stares straight back at him. "I *am* one of those long-haired young folks holding signs outside the meatpackers. In fact, sometimes I lead the protests."

"Yeah?"

"Yeah. I'm a member of AETH."

"What's AETH?"

"Arachneans for the Ethical Treatment of Humans. We believe any mistreatment of humans is a crime against nature and should be stopped."

This is getting too intense. I jump up. "Would anyone like more juice?"

"Stay where you are. Young man, are you trying to tell me that I commit 'crimes against nature'?"

"I'm sorry, sir, I don't mean to offend you or your family, but it's my belief that eating human meat is cruel and morally wrong."

"So…my family and I are morally wrong?"

"In my belief, yes."

"Why?" Dad's voice is deadly calm.

"Do you have any idea where that steak on your grill comes from?"

"From the grocery store. Cheap, too."

"Then it probably came from a factory farm."

"What's a factory farm?"

"Factory farms are death houses. Humans are stood upright in stalls all day so their meat is tender when they're finally slaughtered –"

"Hey, hold on, we're about to eat here."

Pel's voice was quiet. "You know that water in their eyes? That means they're sad."

"Nah, that's just a reflex. Humans don't have feelings."

"Um, sir? Yes, they do."

"Well, the minister at our church says they don't."

I shoot forth an agitated laugh. "I think God has greater matters to concern Herself with than whether or not humans have feelings."

"They do." Pel's voice is low and serious.

"Know that for a fact?" My father gazes directly at him with all of his eyes.

"Yes, sir." They stare each other down.

"I'm gonna need another drink."

"I'm sorry if this is unpalatable to you, but Arachneans need to know this."

"*I* don't need to know! Otherwise, how am I supposed to eat my dinner?"

"Well, I brought extra portabella mushrooms. You can have one if you want."

Dad's mouth twitches. I think I see a slight smile at the corners. "Well, at least let me pour you a drink. It's vegan." He takes a swig of his martini with one hand, reaches for the vodka bottle with another, and picks up a glass with a third. With his fourth, he waves to my mother. "Matti! How're those steaks coming?"

"Almost done!" My mom's cheerful voice resounds from the opposite corner of the patio.

"Any more room on that grill?"

"Why?"

Dad's voice goes up in pitch. The emphasis is poignant. "Pel's a *vegan.*"

"A what?"

"He doesn't eat meat."

"What kind of idiot doesn't eat meat?"

"A *vegan.*" You can tell Dad's using the word as an insult and hoping it'll go over our heads.

Pel gets up. "Sir, I don't mean to cause any trouble. I'll go." He nods stiffly and walks toward the gate.

I follow. "Pel, no. Please. Don't leave."

"I'm sorry. I don't think this is going well." He doesn't even look at me. I can tell he's angry.

"I'm so sorry. Please stay."

His expression softens just a little. He kisses my forehead. "See you in school tomorrow."

I stare at the constellation Palm Tree as I wonder what Pel thinks of me after the barbecue. I remember my favourite dish: pan-seared rump steak, from grain-fed humans, with garden-fresh herbs. You can suck life straight out of it.

My mind wanders to how Pel gagged when he saw the rump steak my mom was serving tonight. Does he now gag when he sees me? Or when he thinks of me?

What am I really concerned with here? And what should I be concerned with?

My little brother Gorkon drops from the ceiling. I jump. "What's shaking, big sister?"

"Go away."

"Why are you wandering around like a drunk bat? Faking so you don't have to go on MindNet for the test tomorrow?" He hangs by a web thread from the kitchen ceiling, using another web thread to bounce a ball on the floor. *I wish he'd spin his web in the bathroom like a grownup. He's such a brat.*

"Go *away.*"

"Okay." He bounces the ball toward me. I catch it and whip it back at him, but he's already gone.

I think of how nimble my mother was when she flipped the steak onto the plates. How deftly she handled the hoisin sauce. The kind of liquid clothing that was put on the poor naked meat.

I gag when I see seafood. I don't think we were ever meant to eat anything that comes out of the water. Those little shrimps are ugly and pink. At least they have exoskeletons, not those squishy disgusting bodies humans have.

I wander back to the kitchen and take a cookbook off the shelf. It's *365 Days of Human* by that famous chef on the Food Channel, and I randomly open it to a page. It's a rump roast. Asses seem to be the theme of the evening. I certainly feel like one after tonight.

Rump roast has always been one of my favourite dishes. It's so easy to suck the blood out of it. Succulent – that's the word that best describes it. I always go right to sleep after a rump roast meal.

Not tonight.

Pel's right. Isn't he? They do have feelings, right?

Mom could be right, too. We still have to liquefy our food; maybe we still have to eat meat. Maybe we're not so evolved after all.

I clap the book shut and grit my fangs. I'm going to go on MindNet tonight and order a vegan cookbook.

"Hey, lovebug." Pel's voice in my head is a welcome relief. It's the next night, and Pel wasn't in school today.

"Hey."

"How'd you do on the test?"

"Probably okay, for once. Thanks to you. You weren't in school today."

"I went to a demonstration."

"Great. That's great." I thought of how my dad would react.

"What's wrong?"

"My parents. They don't understand either of us."

"You know I'm not trying to influence you."

I close my eyes to see him on MindNet. "What are you eating?"

"Tofu sautéed in balsamic, with ramen, kale chips and orange slices."

He shows me a mind-picture of his mom cooking the meal in a wok. I fiddle with a couple of knobs on my helmet, and I can smell the aroma of balsamic tofu and sesame seeds wafting through his kitchen.

"Oh, Pel, that smells delicious!"

"Yep. And it's guilt-free." By this time, Pel is sitting at his desk. I can see his food liquefier behind his head.

"My mom's cooking my favourite meal. Rump steak."

"Ah. Your mom. What a lovely woman."

"She's not that bad. Oh, wait, yes she is." We share a laugh.

Pel's eyebrows go up. "Want to go to a *real* dinner party?"

"I'm intrigued."

He gets up from his desk. "Take my hands." I do. He waves an arm in a dramatic gesture, like a wizard in a fantasy tale. "Behold."

Voices waft across the hills, rising in perfect unison. The sound is new, strange, intensely pleasant. I take a deep breath and open my eyes.

All the colours of the spectrum swirl around me. The grass is greener than any grass I've known. This sky is a deep, brilliant blue awash with golden sunlight.

I'm standing in a great valley, larger than any in my normal world. I look around at the mountains in the distance. Closer to me, Arachneans crouch on hillocks, on trees and on hammocks. Small herds of humans lie on the grass. Bizarrely, they're wearing clothes, and they're holding full glasses, frosted with condensation, in their multi-fingered hands.

Wow, humans' hands are gross. I mean, what do they need all those wiggly little fingers for? And yet, somehow, these humans' hands don't scare me.

Pel lies on his side in a hammock, holding a drink. He motions for me to crouch on the hammock beside him. I do.

"Where am I?"

Pel smiles. "Welcome to Shambhala."

"Is this a real place?"

I hear an unfamiliar voice. "Very real. We create it with our minds, together."

I turn to face a white-haired human, who's grinning with all his ivory teeth exposed. Oddly, he wears two-legged jeans and a tie-dyed shirt. He holds out a drink to me. I look at him harder and recognize him. "Snuffy?"

"Here. Drink this."

I take it and suck in the most delectable liquid I've ever tasted. In an instant, my whole body feels renewed and strong. I could jump right into a tree.

Just then, a cool mist forms in the sky around us. The mist becomes rain, and it falls softly on my hair and body. I sigh as it washes over me, seeming to cleanse me of all pain and sorrow.

As suddenly as it began, the rain stops. Sunlight beams through a fluffy white cloud, blown around by a gentle breeze.

"Wait." I shake my head, trying to focus. "You're *talking?*"

Snuffy's smile softens. "Oh, yes. We have been talking since time immemorial."

"But – how are you communicating with us in this place? I thought humans weren't capable of mind-talk." Overcoming my squeamishness, I reach out my upper left hand and feel his face. "Are – are you real?"

Pel laughs. "He's real, all right. He's as real as the mess his stall was in when I first got him."

"I wasn't used to such deplorable conditions." Snuffy shoots him a wry smile. "You had no idea how to care for a pet human. You had to run five MindNet searches before you figured it out."

"But I did, didn't I? You certainly have a better life than you did at Atrok Labs."

"Hold on." I glance from one to the other. "I don't understand any of this."

Snuffy closes his eyes and shudders. "They used to pour chemicals in my eyes. In the real world, if you can call such horror real, I'm blind."

"But how are you here?"

"I'm one of a special group of humans, Roka. We're capable of telepathy with each other. Pel is one of an equally special, though rarer, group of Arachneans who know of us and have reached out to us."

I take this in. *Pel mind-talks to humans? I wonder how my mother would react.*

"Once in a while, an Arachnean is born with exceptional kindness and awareness, enough to know that all creatures have a soul. They dare to defy convention, to risk being labeled naïve or crazy, and they reach out to us with their minds. They find humans who are able and willing to communicate with them. Then we invite them into our secret realm." Snuffy gestures proudly at the field, the mountains in the distance, and the deep blue sky bathed in sunshine.

The voices build around us, and I listen in rapture. "Those voices – they're strange. They're all individual, but they work together. What *is* this?"

Pel grins widely. "Music. The different voices working together is called harmony. And they're not all voices. Some are instruments. Hear that twanging? That's called a guitar."

"It's – delicious." I honestly can't think of any other word. "What is that language?"

"An ancient human one. It's called 'English'."

Pel takes my hand. We lock arms, both upper and lower, and he twirls me around and around as his voice lightens. "You have flowers in your eyes."

I jerk away from him. "Pel – what are you doing?"

"Dancing with you."

"What's dancing?"

"Remember Junior Float Party at school? This is what humans do instead of hovering in the air staring at each other."

Okay, this makes more sense. "You're so silly."

"But in a charming way, right?" He takes my hands again and gazes at me.

"Right."

I look back into his upper eyes, and we fall into each other's arms for a long moment.

Snuffy's voice breaks the silence. "This is sweet, you two. But I have some wisdom to impart. Will you young lovers listen to me?"

I don't want the moment to end, but Pel gradually releases my hands. Arms in arms, we crouch on the hammock and turn toward Snuffy. We listen as he begins his tale.

"Hundreds of thousands of years ago, Arachneans as they are now didn't exist."

"Yes! We evolved from spiders." I'm eager to show off my knowledge.

"Impressive that you know that. But did you also know humans used to rule the earth?"

"Sort of. But how could they? They're not intelligent."

Snuffy laughs. "We were much more evolved than we are now. We lost our sophisticated physical makeup in the Great Destruction."

"The Great Destruction?"

"Toward the end of our reign, there was so much war, anger and hatred that we used the ultimate weapon. Nuclear bombs. We nearly destroyed the planet. By the time the wars were over, the air was unbreathable. A few of us burrowed underground to save ourselves. There, we lost touch with each other. We no longer had our technology. Over the millennia, we devolved into the species you see today."

"And spiders – Arachneans – survived and evolved." Pel speaks softly. "We got bigger, and humans got smaller. Our lifespans increased while theirs decreased."

"And our lifespans are even shorter now." Snuffy's voice has gone dark. "Just as humans used to do to other 'lower' species, Arachneans now exploit us for what our bodies can give them."

Okay, now I'm skeptical. "How do you know all this?" Still I can't take any of my eyes off him.

"Some of us humans are telepathic. Mind-talkers." He throws me an indulgent glance. "We evolved that ability because so many of us were isolated underground. Those who could mind-talk were able to withstand the isolation and thrive and reproduce."

"So, you've preserved your history somehow through telepathy?"

"There's an oral tradition of sorts that we've handed down through the generations. I even know where my family came from. My name, for example. It's Duncan O'Neill. Surname last, given name first."

"Tulaybon Roka." *Is this really the time for me to introduce myself?*

"Yes," Pel whispers. "When I first got him, I thought 'Snuffy' was –"

"A cute name? Because I have a nose? I suppose your heart was in the right place."

"Yours isn't. It's in your chest." Pel manages a smile.

A realization dawns on me. "Duncan – do *we* look strange to *you?* As strange as you look to us?"

Duncan strokes his beard thoughtfully. "To most of us, yes. But I have to tell you that most humans have an inborn fear of spiders. Millennia ago, there were spiders who were poisonous to humans, and we evolved to fear you. I suppose…everyone fears that which is different."

"But do you fear Arachneans as we are now?"

"Not as much. You're not as hairy." He smiles. "And you look a little like something from our ancient mythology. Something we used to call 'centaurs'. So we've gotten used to you. Except for your multiple eyes." He winks.

"Why are you telling us all this?" The question has been burning in my mind for several minutes.

"Because you need to know. You need to know that humans are valuable beings, worthy of compassion and respect."

"All humans? Even the stupid feral ones?"

"Even them."

"Which means I shouldn't eat you anymore."

"Precisely."

"I don't know. Do I have to give up everything? Pan-seared rump roast? Salt-and-vinegar moth-wing chips?"

"You don't *have* to. I would hope you'd *want* to."

"No way!" I stand. "No way I'm giving up meat. That's crazy! Pan-seared rump roast is my favourite dish. My mom cooks it specially for me!" *I've had enough.* I turn to go.

Duncan sighs and drops his head. He waves his hand.

I'm standing in a building, with creaking and whirring noises all around. It feels stifled and claustrophobic. Duncan and Pel are on either side of me as I stare in horror.

On a conveyor belt, with chains around their hands and feet, are young humans, naked and filthy, with tears in their eyes. Children and adolescents, all with their eyes fixed straight ahead.

At the end of the conveyor belt is a guillotine. One by one, robotic hands push the humans so that they lie on their backs. A robot hand holds them down by the hair, and the guillotine snaps down and severs their heads.

"They put them on their backs so that the cut to the neck will be clean and even," Pel whispers. Duncan shakes his head and wipes his eyes.

The silence is mechanical and droning, broken only by the rhythmic chopping of the blade.

Pel nudges me. "Turn around."

I'm standing in a puddle of urine. Reflexively, I pull my front feet up.

"Look up."

Before me is a line of naked females, mostly adolescents, but some slightly older. They have wires going into their shoulders, tubes running into their vaginas, and pumps on their breasts. They're standing in their own urine and feces.

"These women are artificially inseminated every ten months so that they're always giving milk." Although Pel speaks gently, I can hear the revulsion in his voice.

"What are those wires?"

"Hormone shots."

I swallow hard. *I don't want to know this.* "Pel…what do they do with the old ones? The ones that can't give milk anymore?"

Duncan's face is set, showing all the collective pain his species has endured over the ages. He waves his hand again.

I'm standing on a bridge overlooking a giant pool. Naked older females are squished together in the pool, crammed in, with barely enough room to move.

A blue liquid starts gushing into the pool from pipes coming out of the walls. Steam rises from its surface. The females scream in agony.

I bury my head in Pel's shoulder. His voice is gentle. "They're boiled alive in chemicals. That way, their skin falls off a lot more easily and their bones can be ground up for gelatin. That's what you have in your jelly desserts."

"I can't watch any more!" I burrow my forehead into him. My heart is pounding out of my back.

As the screams fade into birdcalls, I feel a soft breeze on my arms and a light touch on my head. I look up to see Duncan, framed by the distant mountains. We're back in Shambhala.

"Duncan," I whisper, "why haven't the humans done anything about this?"

"What could we do?"

"You could rise up! You could take back your world!" I'm breathless, and I don't know exactly what I'm saying. All I know is that what I've just seen is wrong. My whole world is wrong now.

Duncan walks away and stares at the horizon. "We can't. There aren't enough of us."

"What are you talking about? There are so many of you!"

"Not ones that can mind-talk," Pel says gently. "And even they can't do it because they're not violent. It would never occur to them."

I stand dumbstruck. I feel a wave of shame for what I am.

Duncan walks back to me. "Now do you understand?"

"Yes – yes. I won't eat meat anymore."

"Thank you. Tell others."

I nod and close my eyes.

"Are you all right?" My mom reaches out an upper hand and feels my forehead.

"I'm fine, Mom. Don't hover."

My mom bristles. "I'm not hovering. I'm concerned. This isn't like you."

"Maybe that's a good thing. Change is part of growing up."

My mom crouches on her stool at the kitchen table beside me. "Honey, are you taking drugs?"

Gorkon, who has been listening at the door, pokes his head in and laughs. "She acts like it!"

"Mom! No. I'm just not going to eat meat anymore. Meat is murder."

Her lips purse. "It's that Pel kid, isn't it? He got to you."

"It's not Pel. Well, not entirely. It's the principle of the thing."

"Roka. I understand. When I was your age, I did all kinds of crazy things for boys. But he has to like you for who you are, not who you think he wants you to be."

"Mom! I told you it's not him. It's my own decision."

She ignores me. "When I was in high school, there was a boy who loved cars. He was always working on them. He always had to have the biggest and best motors, steering, snazzy paint jobs. I adored him."

"Again, meat is murder, Mom."

"I begged my parents for a sportscar just so he could work on it."

"Mom! Mom! Listen to me! Don't you understand? Humans have feelings."

"How do you know?"

"I—I don't know how I know! I just do!" My right central eye tic is pulsing furiously.

"Okay." Gorkon scuttles over to the table and hunkers down. "You know what goes on in forests, right? We cut down trees to make our shelters. What about wheat fields? We use combines to harvest wheat. We cut it right off. Don't you think that hurts it? What about the poor wheat?"

I stare straight ahead. "There's no evidence that plants feel pain. Humans do."

"So what? Life is pain, big sister. We all have to deal with it."

This is getting me nowhere. "I'm going up to my room."

My mom softens her voice. "Okay. Just in case you're interested, remember I'm pan-searing rump steak tonight."

"Whatever, Mom." I'm walking away.

"With garden-fresh herbs."

"Okay." I'm halfway up the stairs.

"From grain-fed humans!" Her voice is far off in the distance by now.

"I don't know what's happening to my world," I say to Pel as he strokes my arms.

"Don't stress, lovebug." Pel soothes me.

"Roka!" My mother knocks on my door and then enters. I snap out of MindNet.

"Hi, Mom." *Reality just arrived.*

She shuffles her way through the mess of moth-wing chip bags all over my floor, brushing them out of the way. She sets a steaming plate of rump roast on my desk. "Now, you don't have to eat it, sweetie. I know you're sensitive, and it's good that you're learning new things. I just didn't want to exclude you from dinner."

Oh God. She's decorated it with garden-fresh herbs in the shape of a smiley face.

"Thanks, Mom."

"Bon appetite." She smiles as she gently closes my door.

I run to the bathroom and throw up. Then I dump my dinner in the toilet and flush it all down.

"Why is your face so pale?" Trust Gorkon to point this out to my parents. As usual, he's being a whiny brat.

"Yes, Roka, why *is* your face so pale?" My mother flips burgers on the grill. I suck on the one she's just cooked for me, a cheap meat substitute that tastes like it's made of salt.

Dad picked it up at the discount grocery store last week.

"I don't know. I guess I got some kind of bug at Senior Float."

"Probably caught it from that Pel kid." I can *feel* the disdain in Dad's voice.

"I bet someone spiked the punch."

"Shut *up*, Gorkon."

I've been a full vegan for two weeks now. My parents don't like it, but they can't force dead human down my throat. Grudgingly, my dad now stops by the vegan grocery store when it's convenient, but he usually picks up fake meat from the discount place.

"Are you all right, sweetie?" Dad leaps up and puts a hand under my left arms. Mom drops her spatula and rushes over.

Suddenly the world seems vague, whirling, fading. Like I'm a thousand miles away.

"I don't know. I need…"

I collapse on the ground in a heap.

"She'll be fine." Doctor Baluka hangs her stethoscope back around her neck. "She just needs a fresh infusion of blood."

"She's been in a vegan phase." My mom lets out a nervous laugh. Her voice drops to a whisper. "It's this boy she met at school. He's a bad influence."

"I understand." The doctor takes a prescription pad from her pocket. "Actually, I have several patients who are vegans. There's nothing wrong with it as an ideology, but unfortunately we live in the real world." She turns to me. "And in the real world, you need protein and iron. Things you can only get from human blood. Do you understand?"

"No! Meat is murder. I've seen it myself!"

"I'm sure you have, dear. And I commend you for trying to be compassionate. But you need to think of your health first."

"I don't care. I'm not going to eat meat again. Ever."

The doctor purses her lips. "Tell you what. I'm going to write you a prescription." She writes something and tears off a page and hands it to me. "Take one of these every morning. It's a protein and iron supplement. It should take care of the fainting spells."

"Okay. Thank you, doctor."

"Good luck, dear."

"Hey lovebug. Feeling any better?"

"A little."

"Taking the supplement that doctor gave you?"

"Yeah." I glance at the bottle of red gel caps on my desk.

"Atrok Labs?"

"Yes. How did you know?"

"Lucky guess. Duncan knows them well."

I don't want to know this either. "Oh my God. That's where he came from!"

Pel's face curls into a smile. "Come with me."

I close my eyes, and open them in the familiar valley. I'm in Shambhala again.

"Feel better, bug?"

"No! Everywhere you look in my world, there's cruelty. My shampoo? Tested on humans. My clothes? Leather jacket, suede shoes. Cruelty!" I bury my head in my upper arms.

"Relax, Roka." I look up to see Duncan smiling at me.

"Oh, Duncan…I'm so sorry." Out of everyone I know, Duncan is the one from whom I need forgiveness the most. If I were a human, I'd be sobbing right now.

"It's not your fault."

"But…I'm not sure I can be a vegan."

"Perhaps not. But there are other things you can do."

"We Arachneans evolved from spiders." Pel takes one of my hands in his and covers it with another of his hands. "They were obligate carnivores."

"Some of them ate veggies." I remember this from my MindNet research. My parents certainly wouldn't have wanted me to know that.

"Mostly, they drank blood. Some larger species ate some veggies, but they still had to rely on blood for their nutrition."

"I guess so…."

"Over the millennia, we evolved, and most of us grew longer digestive tracts. That makes it possible for us to process vegetables. But every now and then, someone is born without everything they need in order to do that." Pel pauses. I can see he's unsure how to tell me this. "You may need to face the fact that you're not physically capable of being a complete vegan."

"I have to be!"

"I know a place where you can get human blood."

"But…isn't that cruel? Don't they line the humans up with IV poles or something?"

Pel laughs and gestures to the nearby groups of humans in the field. "No. See these humans? They volunteer there. They donate their blood."

This is definitely getting weird. "Volunteer?"

"Yes." Duncan speaks softly. "We know many of you can't survive without our help. So we came up with a solution. A few of us go to Motrey Clinic every couple of months to donate our blood."

"Right out in the open? Aren't you afraid word will get out about mind-talking humans?"

"We do it discreetly. In the public eye, Motrey Clinic brands itself as a free-range blood farm. A small group of telepathic humans actually allow themselves to be trapped and taken in to give our blood. That way, it appears to the casual observer that they're simply wandering feral humans who are bled and released. Very few Arachneans know that they do it voluntarily."

"It's still icky." I honestly can't think of another word for it.

"It might be necessary for you." Duncan looks thoughtful. "Consider yourself lucky. When we humans dominated the earth, animals didn't have the ability to make these decisions. We simply exploited them for our own convenience."

I crouch on a stool in the waiting room. Pel sits beside me, thumbing through a magazine.

"Tulaybon Roka?" The admitting nurse is a small, perky little guy in heels, wearing pants that accentuate his bulbous spinnerets. "Come in please." He swishes around and leaves, his shoes clicking on the floor.

Pel and I amble in and I lie on the hammock. Pel crouches on one of the stools near Doctor Baluka's desk.

"You didn't have to come with me."

"Yes I did. You're my girlfriend. I support you."

The doctor rushes in, holding a clipboard in her left hands.

"How are you feeling today?"

"A little better. Thanks, doc."

"I have your lab results back. I regret to tell you that it's as we suspected. You don't have the enzyme necessary to synthesize iron on a meat-free diet."

Pel says, "What about other options?"

"There are no other options. Roka has to eat meat." She sees the expression on Pel's face and eyes him up and down. "I don't want to disparage anyone's beliefs here, but we have to be realistic."

"I'm taking her to Motrey Clinic."

"You can certainly go that route. I understand they treat the humans humanely and that's commendable. But I can give no guarantee that Roka's health will improve on extracted human blood."

"We'll give it a try."

"Doctor, is there a problem with extracted blood?" *Oh, God, I don't want to know this.*

"The Blood and Drug Administration hasn't approved it. For a very good reason. There's no hard evidence that shows that extracted blood, which has been out of the human body for days or weeks, is effective when consumed by iron-deficient vegans. And let me add, despite what you read on fringe websites, there's also no hard evidence that insentient humans 'volunteer' their services for these places."

She puts down her pen and looks me straight in the central eyes. "Look, Roka, I sympathize. I truly do. I've had many patients like you who don't want to eat meat, and believe me, I know what goes on in the meat industry. But there are certain realities we all must face. It would be nice if we all lived in an ideal world, but we don't."

"Roka, you know we love you and we only want the best for you." My mom crouches on the stool beside me, stroking my face. We're in the kitchen having a light dinner, and the bare bulb on the ceiling casts a harsh light on the stove, the fridge, and the dishwasher.

"I know, Mom."

"Speak for yourself!" Gorkon slurps his meal.

"It's nice that you're such a kind person. That you want to avoid hurting the humans. But what we're *trying* to get across to you is that *this doesn't hurt them*. Humans don't feel emotions like we do. Not at all. You're anthropomorphizing dumb animals."

Useless to argue. "Okay."

"So here. Rump roast. Your favourite." She triumphantly cuts off a piece with a knife and fork and places the fork close to the smell sensors on my arm.

My heart feels heavy, like it's about to drop from my back into my left spinneret. I pick up the fork.

As I suck on the meat, I feel as if I just ordered Duncan to the guillotine.

"Don't worry, lovebug." Pel's voice is gentle, but a little distant. "It'll be all right. We'll figure something out."

"I'll try again. It was just a little setback."

"You might not be able to try again soon."

"I know. With my bougie parents in the mix."

"Well, that and your health issues."

"You know what? I'm not even sure they're real. I'm going to try that blood bank."

"Good choice." I open my eyes to face Duncan. The cool valley breeze washes over my face.

"Roka, you're a kind soul. You may not realize it, but your kindness is an influence on others."

"Not on my parents."

"Yes, on them. They're thinking about it." He smiles. "That's all we're asking you to do."

Pel hands me a tofu bar on a stick. He hands one to Duncan as well, and crouches down and begins to devour a third.

As we watch the sun sink lower behind a mountain, a whisper of rain grows around us. We become one with the glowing sunset sky, one with each other. The mists of Shambhala waft over our faces, washing away our sorrow and shame.

"Duncan…can you ever forgive me?"

"That's not up to me. Can you forgive yourself?"

I honestly don't know. "I can try."

Naomi Vondell is a Canadian writer living in Thunder Bay, Canada. She is passionate about animal rights and spends her time in nature, reading, writing, and gathering story ideas.

Snakeflower
Natalie Dale

The tavern is crowded, even for a triple crescent. Like most buildings on Ilaria, it has no roof, and on clear nights like this, I can see the three moons that determine the rhythm of our lives. A triple crescent, though not unusual, is the luckiest combination of moon-states. That's why I chose tonight. I'm going to need all the luck I can get.

Raucous conversation echoes through the clearing, the smell of stale ale and sweat permeating the humid jungle air. A group of men play dice in one corner, their yells growing louder with each toss. They wear plain clothes – brown trousers and loose shirts unbuttoned to show tangles of chest hair – but their heads are shaved in the manner of UIF soldiers. One even wears the blue and gold armband. The other patrons give the men a wide berth. No one wants to anger the UIF. Not anymore.

A metal cup slides down the bar and nearly hits me in the elbow. I glare at the bartender – a tall, lanky man named Kiso – as he wipes out a mug with a filthy rag.

"You need a drink," he says in heavily accented Föder. "You look stupid sitting in a bar without a drink."

"Thanks," I reply, careful to hide my own accent. It's been years since it was legal to speak my native Maayu, and I do not want anyone questioning my presence here. Instead, I lift the mug to my nose and sniff. It's just yucca beer with a bit of yeast added, hardly intoxicating, but the smell is enough to clear my sinuses.

"You ready?" Kiso asks, his voice low as he leans close.

I take a long drink of the amber liquid, force my fingers to stop their incessant drumming against the wooden bar.

"I don't know what you're talking about."

Kiso smiles and straightens, tugging on a long, drooping earlobe that betrays his native blood. He told me once that his transparency was his armor. That by looking, dressing, and speaking like a riverman, then docilely serving UIF soldiers, they overlook him. Underestimate him. I doubt that I could ever be so brazen.

One of the soldiers stands, shaking his head. The other men are cat-calling, goading him, but he laughs good-naturedly as he starts for the bar.

"Kasha help me, I need ten snakeyes," he says, taking the empty stool beside me. His speech is crisp and terse, as if every consonant were spat from his lips. Even more than his uniform, his accent marks him as hailing from one of the inner planets of the Federation. Tall and muscular, his pale, bald head gleams pale green light of *Qilla*, our first and brightest moon. He could be anyone; any soldier in the UIF, at least. But then he turns towards me, his gray eyes dead as the fish that float belly-up after the spawn, and I know it's him. Every hair on my body stands to attention.

You've got a job to do, I remind myself, *don't get distracted.*

But I can't stop the bile rising at the back of my throat. Suddenly, I'm back, cowering in the shallows beneath the riverhouse, the smell of cauterized flesh searing my nostrils. I begin to tremble, though whether from fear or rage, I'm not quite sure.

"You sure you can pay for that?" Kiso's voice drags me back to the present.

The soldier smirks and tosses a thin copper disk imprinted with the sigil of the Federation onto the bar.

"That should about cover it."

Without waiting for Kiso's reaction, the man turns back to me. His cold eyes linger on the swell of my breasts rising above the lacing of my leather vest and I suppress a shudder. I hate these clothes – the short leather skirt and the tight vest meant to make me look like a *broija* ripe for the picking – but his eyes make me feel as if I'm wearing nothing at all.

"What's a pretty girl like you doing in a place like this?"

I force myself to take a deep breath. *The mission.* It requires all my training to smile, reach up and smooth my black hair, making sure it covers my ears.

"Waiting for friends," I say, knocking back to the rest of my drink. It tastes awful, but I just smile and tip the empty cup towards him. "But I could use a refill in the meantime."

He hesitates, runs a finger over the dark stubble of his jaw. Then Kiso sets a tray with ten glasses – real glass – brimming with a thin white liquid, in front of him.

"Sorry," the soldier says with a wink, "can't let the boys get thirsty."

I watch him weave through the crowd, balancing the heavy tray easily, a knot solidifying in my gut. I can't decide if I'm relieved or disappointed. I've been training for tonight for months; I can't let anything stand in my way. Not even vengeance.

"Don't take it personal, sweetheart," Kiso says, pouring a drink for a man with a thin gray braid trailing down his back, "them UIF boys aren't too keen on strangers lately."

He doesn't know, of course. How could he? To him, I'm just another recruit bungling my first mission. How could he know that the man who'd carried out the murder of my family was sitting the next booth over. The man with the braid looks over.

"Not keen on strangers?" he asks, his voice already slurred despite the early hour, "They're terrified of this new resistance. Command won't let them go anywhere unless they're in a group of at least four."

Dragging myself back to the present, I frown, feigning confusion.

"Resistance?" I ask, in my highest, most girlish voice, "but the war is over. The United Intergalactic Federation won."

The man twitches his nose.

"Some folk seem to have a hard time grasping that."

I nod, but the knot in my gut is pulling tighter. I've been here for less than an hour, but I'm already floundering. The mission is an easy one; lure a low-ranking soldier out back, then slip him a few drops qichap oil – just enough that he'll answer when I ask when the next shipment of palladium is due to leave, but not enough that he passes out. Then I pick up where we left off, and he returns to his friends with nothing but memories of stolen kisses and a pounding headache that he will attribute to too many snakeyes. My superiors pointed out that it would be easier to just kill him – then there would be no possibility of the qichap oil wearing off too soon, or the dose being insufficient to wipe his memory. But I'd refused. Riverfolk do not kill.

I turn slightly, watching the soldiers from the corner of my eye. They're a tight knit group: no castoffs, no loners. No easy mark. The grey-eyed soldier sits at their center, his companions orbiting him like moons, pulled close by the force of his personality. He is handsome and generous with his money, his laugh loud and raucous. But his mirth never reaches his eyes.

I down the rest of my drink and stand. I can't just keep sitting here, waiting for something to happen. It's time for me to make my move.

"Off already?" Kiso asks. His voice is light and casual, but I can tell he's worried. Command put me in his charge, after all. To make sure I don't bungle things too badly. I'm allowed to get myself killed, but Kiso has strict orders not to let me do anything that might damage the resistance.

I shake my head.

"Just getting lonely."

Without waiting for a reply, I head straight for the soldiers. They fall silent as I approach.

"My friends are very late," I say, slurring my words and perching unsteadily on the back of a chair at the table beside theirs, "and I'm bored. Does anyone want to buy me a drink?"

Every head turns towards the grey-eyed soldier. His eyes burn into me as he looks me up and down.

"Sorry," he says, his voice curt, "we don't need your kind around here."

My heart stumbles, and I bite my lip to keep from crying out. How could he possibly know…?

But the other men are staring at me hungrily. One of them has opened his belt pouch and is hurriedly counting his coins.

Relief floods through me as I realize what he'd meant. I thrust my lower lip into a pout.

"I'm no prostitute," I protest, "I'm a harvester."

I step forward and poke him in his broad chest.

"Now you really owe me a drink."

The other soldiers laugh uproariously.

"She's got a point," one cackles, nearly falling out of his chair.

The soldier sighs exaggeratedly, then stands.

"You're right, of course," he says, "it would be unchivalrous of me to turn you away now. Please, let me buy a drink"

He takes my hand – I have to restrain myself from jerking it away – and leads me to the bar. The gold F on his armband flashes as he hails the bartender, and my stomach curdles.

"I'm Danel," he says, turning back to me. "Jismay."

"So, what do you really do here?" he asks.

I shove down my annoyance.

"I told you. I'm a harvester."

Danel's eyebrows shoot upward.

"No kasha. I didn't think women were allowed in the jungle."

I shrug, trying to act as if I didn't know about the Federation's many new restrictions of the people of Ilaria.

"No one's tried to stop me yet."

Danel leans back, crosses his arms. His eyes rake me up and down, lingering on the swell of my breasts, the gap between my thighs where my skirt has ridden up. I tug it down, and his eyes narrow.

"Then what's your specialty?"

I can tell he doesn't believe me. That he can't imagine a world where a woman could survive alone in the jungle. I turn my attention to the cup in his hands.

"Snakeflower."

Danel drops the cup like it bit him, the thin white liquid sloshing over the sides.

"No way," he says, disbelief thick in his voice, "I've never met anyone who's actually seen one."

I take a long drink, buying time to pull my thoughts together.

"To be fair, most Ilarians have never seen the plant either," I say, "just harvesters."

Danels leans forward, his eyes sparkling, his face transformed by a genuine curiosity.

"I was training as a botanist back home, before – well, before I got conscripted. I read the plant has some unusual properties," he says excitedly, "like if you burn it, it's supposed to –

"We'd never burn it," I say quickly, "it's too valuable."

Not to mention heretical.

Danel looks down at the cup in his hand, frowning. "Isn't harvesting incredibly dangerous?

I shrug.

"It's not as hard as they make it sound. The thorns on the vine are poisonous, that's where it gets its name."

Danel lifts his cup, holds it up to the light.

"Then they should charge less for it."

I laugh, rest a hand on his forearm. My fingers look so small, so dark, against the milksop white of his skin. I lean in close, my lips grazing his ear.

"Don't tell him that," I whisper, gesturing towards Kiso, "it'd be a shame if my best customer were to realize my product wasn't quite as hazardous as I make it out to be."

Danel shakes his head, downs the rest of his drink, then pulls another sigil-marked disc from his pocket and slams it onto the table.

"Keep them coming, bartender"

He turns back to me, leaning one elbow on the bar as Kiso begins filling the drinks.

"All right, beautiful," he says, leaning forward and resting a cleft chin on the palm of his hand, "tell me about your adventures in the jungle."

Danel's words start slurring as he finishes glass after glass of snakeyes, but his eyes never lose their sharp focus. His calloused thumb creeps under my skirt, rubbing back and forth against the soft skin of my thigh, but despite the many, heavy-handed hints I dropped about finding somewhere quieter, he seems content just to sit and talk. The tavern begins to empty, as Qilla, the first of our three moons, drops below tangled jungle canopy. With every passing moment, I feel my chance slipping through my fingers. Even Kiso is starting to look restless. Then, just as Wallya, our second moon, begins to slip away, one of Danel's compatriots – a short, wiry man with strange, violet eyes – appears behind us.

"Time to go, captain," he says, his voice deep and gruff, "Trinton's lost a whole week's wages and he's angry as a spotted jungle cat."

I start, my pulse accelerating. Danel is not just another soldier. He's their captain.

The UIF doesn't bother with exposure therapy for enlisted troops; there are always more men to conscript. But an officer of Danel's rank will not only have undergone exposure therapy for most of Ilaria's common poisons but will also receive regular serum testing. If I use the qichap oil on him, they will be able to trace it back to me. I've spent the whole night chasing a quarry I'm not allowed to catch.

Danel glances over his shoulder towards his men.

"Kasha," he mutters, "that boy needs to learn how to win."

My stomach twists as he stands, touching the blaster at his hip as if checking to make sure it's still there. I feel the mission slipping through my fingers like fish through a net. If I fail – no. I can't let myself think that way. I have to find a way to salvage this.

"Those are your men?" I ask, infusing my voice with just enough of a quaver to pass for admiration. "All of them?"

Danel's chest puff's out, and he touches his armband.

"Yes," he says, "them and more. I'm the Captain."

I let my jaw fall open, a little gasp escaping my lips. Then I smile up at the second man, repressing a shudder as I meet his violet stare.

"Then this must be your Commander," I say, slipping off my stool and bending my knees in the absurd gesture the UIF call a curtsey. "I've never met someone of such high rank before."

Danel's expression darkens; the second man's skin blanches.

"This is Alarin," Donel says, his voice pinched, "he's one of mine."

My fingers fly to my lips, and I widen my eyes.

"Oh," I say, looking back and forth between them, "I'm sorry. I just thought because he was giving you orders."

Danel's eyes flash. Behind him, I see Kiso touch a finger to his nose in admiration.

"I give the orders here," Danel snaps. "Alarin, take the men back to the barracks."

The wiry man paled further.

"But Captain, Command specifically said…"

Danel reaches down and pulls his blaster from the holster, holding it up to the light as if admiring it. The tavern falls suddenly, completely silent.

"I am a Level 7 weapons holder," he says, turning the weapon over and over in his hands, "I don't need to travel in a pack like some mangy cur."

Suddenly, his other arm is around my waist, his fingers digging into the bare skin where my vest meets my skirt. I have to grit my teeth not to shove him away.

"I'm not going anywhere," he says, his voice deadly calm, "but you and the boys are going back to the barracks. Sound fair?"

He cocks the blaster absently, not quite pointing it at the other man. It makes a low hum as it powers up.

Alarin nods furiously, snaps a salute.

"Yes, Captain."

The men leave without finishing their drinks. I watch them go, a sinking feeling in the pit of my stomach. But Danel's grip doesn't loosen from my waist. He stands at attention, glowering at his men until the door to the tavern slaps shut behind them. Then he slams another copper disk onto the bar.

"Let's get out of here," he growls.

I try to hesitate, ask if he'll buy me just one more drink, but he's dragging me towards the exit, his hand so tight on my wrist I know I'll sport finger-shaped bruise tomorrow. I only have the chance to throw one, pleading glance back towards Kiso, before I'm towed through the door and out into the humid jungle night.

"You got a cabin around here or anything?" Danel asks, his voice slurred.

I shake my head.

"I live with my family," I say, "there's quite a lot of us. We all sleep in one room."

That used to be true, at least.

Danel frowns, shakes his head at the stupidity of the natives. Then he glares down the road toward the low, long buildings that house the soldiers. Even at this hour, the road leading to the spaceport is well-traveled. I can see at least four men in UIF armor patrolling, while AI-controlled hovercarts flit past at astonishing speeds. Behind us, the ancient diesel generator that powers the tavern coughs and sputters.

Danel's grip tightens around my waist, and he makes as if to start down the street towards the barracks, then stops abruptly, eying the soldiers. It's strictly forbidden for a soldier to bring a civilian into the barracks – a demotion level offense – but Donel looks like he's seriously considering it anyway. I shudder, imagining what he would do if he got me alone in his bunk. Then I remember what he did to my sisters and I think I might throw up.

"I do know somewhere we can go," I say quickly, "somewhere we can be alone."

I immediately regret saying anything. He's a level 7 weapons carrier; I am armed with a useless vial of qichap oil. I was supposed to stay in the bar, within earshot of Kiso should anything go wrong. This man is dangerous; I have seen what he is capable of.

And just like that, I'm under the riverhouse again, watching the mangled bodies of my brothers and sisters splash into the murky brown water, the Federation's sigil burned into their eyelids. I can hear his boots on the floorboards above me, feel the utter terror when his dead eyes look straight at me and I'm sure I've been found. Part of me wants to be found, to join my siblings in death. But another part dreams of stealing his blaster and taking down every last soldier that obliterated our riverhouse and murdered my family in order to steal our palladium-rich land.

But riverfolk do not kill.

I shake my head, pulling myself back to the present. I'd joined the resistance as a spy. My purpose is to glean information; trick soldiers into telling me what I need to know. I never dreamed I would come face to face with the man responsible for my family's murder. That I would have the chance to get him alone.

Donel raises an eyebrow, looks me up and down.

"How alone?"

I know what I have to do. I lift up on my tiptoes, let my lips graze my ear.

"Very alone."

I force my fingers to linger on hollow notch at the base of his throat, lick my bottom lip as I stare up at him. His dead eyes gaze down at me, unreadable. But his breath has quickened, and I can feel him leaning towards me.

Danel smiles – a wide, satisfied smile, like a jungle cat with its next meal trapped between his paws. I'm suddenly afraid, terrified that I've made the wrong decision.

"Lead the way."

I take his hand and start down the path leading away from the tavern. Cement turns to dirt beneath our feet, and I can see the tangled dark of the jungle, smell its earthy aroma, before he finally stops, planting his feet so hard my arm is nearly jerked from my socket.

"The jungle?"

The tiny quaver of fear in his voice sends a thrill of pride up my spine.

"Of course," I say, "where else?"

Danel's eyes narrow. Then, quick as a fish, he's pulled his blaster, aiming it at my chest.

"Why should I go into the jungle with you," he snaps, all trace of slur gone from his voice, "you could be leading me into a trap."

I stare at him, frozen with horror. Not knowing what else to do, I reach up and tuck my hair back behind my long drooping ears. Danel's eyes widen, but the barrel of the blaster remains pointed straight at me.

"You're – you're riverfolk?"

"Yes, you arrogant murderer," I say in Maayu, smiling widely. Then I switch back to Föder, allowing my accent to slip through. "I am. So you know I can't hurt you. It's against our creed."

The tip of his blaster lowers, though he does not take his eyes from me. He knows the riverfolk are pacifists, knows we take up no weapons other than the spears and nets we use to fish. Of course he knows. It's how he slaughtered us so easily.

He gazes into the tangled mess of jungle, his thumb running up and down the trigger.

"It isn't safe at night," he says. "There's jungle cats and all other manner of beasts."

I allow myself a single, lilting laugh.

"It's not so bad," I say, "anyway, I'm with you. I know you'll protect me."

Danel tucks the blaster back into his holster, his former smirk returning to his face.

"You're right there," he says. "There's nothing in there I can't handle."

I tug on his hand again, and this time, he follows. But we only get a few steps before he stops again.

"A light," he says, "I don't have a flasher with me. Both moons are down, and third gives barely any light at all."

This time, my laugh is genuine.

"You really haven't been in the jungle at night, have you?"

He stares at me, brow furrowed. I squeeze his hand and whisper in his ear.

"Trust me."

We start down the path again, pushing past hanging vines and stepping over gnarled roots. Insects buzz, nightbirds call, and in the distance, I can hear the low murmur of my river. I smile, inhale the smell of the damp earth, letting it fill me, renew me. The trees grow closer and denser, blotting out the pale light of Abiha until I can no longer see my brightly beaded sandals.

"This is absurd," Danel mutters, stumbling in the dark. "there's no way…"

And then he sees it – the faint, bluish glow – and he falls silent. We push through a curtain of vines, and he gasps.

Hundreds of blue-green lights burst into existence all around us, seeming to float in the air. Danel's jaw drops open.

"What are they?"

I laugh, my first real life since I went down into the rivercellar all those months ago. It's been so long since I traveled the jungle at night.

"Estrion trees," I say, tilting my face up to the light, "they release strontium aluminate in their flowers at night. Attracts some special kind of insect."

We stand in silence, then Danel steps forward and runs a finger along the vase-shaped flower.

"I didn't know they were real," he says softly, "the books…they.."

He shakes his head, as if waking from a dream.

"They never said it could be like this."

I step forward, interlace my fingers with his. In the pale blue light, with his face tipped upwards and his mouth falling open, he looks years younger. Even his eyes dance. I can hardly believe that this is not the man who led the ambush on my family, the man who raped my sisters and seared the Federation sigil onto their eyelids. But then a macerak chitters and his hand flies to his blaster. My resolve hardens.

"It's not much farther," I say, taking his hand.

We continue down the path, hand in hand. Danel glances from side to side, his eyes wide with amazement as he takes in the estrion flowers, the vines that hang in curtains, the white moths the size of his fist that dance around the flowers.

"I can't believe I've never been in here at night," he says, "it's so beautiful."

I stop, and Danel, still staring up at the glowing canopy, runs straight into me. This section of the forest looks no different from any other; blue-green light bathes the vine covered trunks of trees that soar hundreds of feet into the canopy, their fronds dangling with the bulky, vase-shaped estrion flowers that were the source of that light. I turn, wrap my arms around his waist.

"We're here."

Danel's eyes gleam. Then he leans down and kisses me hard. One hand pushes me tight against him, while the other starts undoing the ties at the front of my vest. I push him away, and for a moment, I worry he'll see the revulsion on my face.

"I thought you wanted to see the snakeflower," I say, too fast.

Danel frowns.

"I'm not really here to see some plant."

He grabs at me again, pulls me hard against him. I let him kiss me, grope my breast like it's an eel he can't quite catch. I can smell the alcohol seeping from his pores, but his hands are steady as he tugs at my skirt. I try to squirm away, but he holds me fast.

"Hold still," he growls, his fingers digging into my shoulder as he presses me against him.

"Wait," I say, "look."

Danel spins, blaster out, a low hum as it powers to life.

"What is it?" he snaps. "Jungle cat?"

I laugh, not sure if I'm relieved or terrified.

"No, silly." It's hard to keep my voice playful, to hide my fear and revulsion. "It's a snakeflower vine."

Danel follows my gaze to a delicate green vine hanging from a gnarled branch overhead. A single white flower, no bigger than my fingernails, perches on the vine, just above a long, thin thorn.

"That's it?" he says, lowering the blaster, "it looks like a blackberry."

I have no idea what a blackberry is, so I just nod.

Danel's eyes are hungry as he takes in the vine.

"We could do so much with this," he says, breathless. "Command thinks they're too dangerous, but if I could bring one back…"

He trails off.

"You said you harvest the flowers?"

My heart pounds. Somehow, I'd always known it would come down to this.

"Yes," I say, "just don't touch the thorns. Even a careless brush can be deadly."

For a moment I worry that he will tell me to do it, that he will overpower me. But he just steps forward and plucks the delicate flower from the vine.

He doesn't have a chance to react. The end of the vine whips out and around, sinking thorns deep into his flesh. The flower drops to forest floor and is crushed under his boot as he stumbles away from the plant. I back away. Even from here, I can see an angry welt forming at the site of the sting.

"You bitch" he spits, "you knew it would do that."

He starts towards me, his hand moving towards his blaster, but I'm faster. Months of training in hand-to-hand combat, years of scurrying through the jungle, surviving on my wits and speed, coalesce into this single moment. Rage courses through me like the river in flood. I dash forward and with one punch, knock the blaster from his hands. My next kick sends him stumbling backwards, slamming into a tree covered with the vines.

They spring to life, the tiny white flowers drifting to the ground as the thorns slam into his flesh. Angry red welts rise on his face, his arms, his neck, anywhere the thorns made contact, the poison finding the quickest route to his heart.

He struggles, fighting the vines that held him, his handsome face growing red and twisted.

"Help," he calls, his throat already swelling with the poison, "help me."

I freeze, suddenly realizing what I've done. I've broken the sacred trust of my people, failed my mission, and jeopardized the entire resistance.

But I don't care. The torrent of rage has ebbed, leaving behind only an icy satisfaction. I step closer, deftly avoiding the twisting mass of thorns to pluck a delicate flower from his shirt.

"Never again."

In 2017, Natalie Dale, MD, took a leap of faith and left the world of medicine to focus on her long-time passion: writing. Her short stories and essays have been published in Breath & Shadow, READ White & Blue Anthology, The Bipolar Battle, and National Alliance on Mental Illness (NAMI). Currently, she is pursuing publication for her debut novel, 'Pathétique' and working on a nonfiction 'Writer's Guide to Medicine.' In her spare time, she organizes an elementary school reading program, runs a local writing critique group, and plays violin in a community orchestra.

To the New Year
Alexandra Grunberg

It was the end of time, and everyone was waiting for the countdown to the New Year.

Louisa stared at the screen in Lord Addleburg's study, a familiar image of a crowded Times Square, and fought the urge to cry, or throw up, or laugh hysterically. She had watched this livestream every year since she was a little girl and she had been so sure that it would be different tonight. The giddy energy of the bundled-up masses should have turned to abject sorrow or riotous panic, but the cheers of the individuals as the camera found their faces were the same as always, the reporters' smiles just as bright. It was like they had all secured their own exclusive ticket out, instead of being the many who were not so lucky. The many for whom this year would be the very last.

It probably did not feel real to them. It did not feel real to her.

Louisa tilted her head back before mascara could drip down her cheeks. It was better than throwing up, or the absurd giggling she could hear from the other rooms. Ten minutes away, said the number at the corner of the screen. Louisa took a deep breath, and the image came into focus as the need to cry passed.

"Louisa!"

She heard Marianne's chipper voice and felt the woman's slim fingers on her shoulders before Louisa saw her. Marianne's lips pressed against her cheek and Louisa tried to find the sensation as pleasant as she usually did. If the way she pushed Marianne away was not entirely playful, her already tipsy girlfriend did not notice.

"How can you watch that?" Marianne asked, sticking out her tongue at Times Square. "It's too depressing."

"I think it's important for us to remember them," said Louisa, trying to memorize the blue pompon on a little boy's hat, the exact colour green of a laughing man's eyes. "I don't know why, but I think I won't feel so bad, afterwards, if I can bring the memory of some stranger with me."

"It's not your fault that they're unlucky," shrugged Marianne.

"They're not unlucky," said Louisa. "Just poor."

Poor compared to them. Poor compared to everyone who could afford a ticket to Lord Addleburg's final New Year's Eve party. Poor compared to Lord Addleburg, who bought his title when he was twenty-eight, and built a city around his sky-scraper of a mansion so there would always be crowds to keep him company, and funded research by the leading and most ambitious scientific minds for reasons he kept to himself.

"Being poor is unlucky and being rich is lucky," said Marianne. "It's just the kind of luck that lasts for generations. You know the story of the butterfly wing? It makes change happen with each flap-flap-flap. Luck is like a butterfly wing of money. It giveth and it taketh away, and we'll never know what our lives could have been like if the butterfly flapped in a different direction. Do you want another cocktail? Your glass is empty."

Sometimes it seemed like Addleburg's occasional parties that Louisa attended and the entertainment news detailing his lovers and adventures were the only parts of an increasingly depressing world that brought her joy. Sure, none of it mattered then, but the things that mattered were too hopeless to focus on for long. Addleburg was a diversion; rich, handsome, perhaps not smart but appreciative of those who were. He was not important, until he was the most important person in the world.

There was no meteor. No terrible climate disaster. No unstoppable war. There was just the knowledge that the world would never get any better, and the human race had a big enough arsenal of nuclear weapons to stop it from getting worse. And Lord Addleburg's scientific minds had come up with an escape route, a doorway of sorts. The Gate. A potential of splintering that just needed an adequate explosion to set it off. And then the partygoers could end up... wherever they wanted. Whenever they wanted. Any time that was preferable to a present lacking a future.

Louisa supposed Lord Addleburg had enough money to bribe the powers that be into complying with his plan, but money was not as important as a ticket. Everyone was eager to leave. Almost everyone. Louisa's parents had declined their tickets, tucking them into their only child's coat pocket before she left. She quietly gave them to a couple who waited in a mass outside of Lord Addleburg's gates, a much more appropriately unhappy mass than the one waiting in Times Square. The woman, wearing a cheap dress and a puffy coat to protect against the lazy snowfall, wrapped her arms around Louisa's neck and cried into her shoulder. The man was shocked into stillness and needed to be led by his wife's hand as they followed Louisa, a giggling Marianne who thought Louisa's generosity was somehow deviant, and the rest of their entourage of loyal sorority sisters and their ex-boyfriends through the gate while the unlucky wailed outside.

The woman who hugged her and cried was standing on her left when Louisa stepped out of the chauffeur's car. There was another couple standing to her right. As heavily armed guards closed the sparkling gates behind them, Louisa could see that couple in the crowd, crying for a very different reason. She could have turned right, but she was left-handed, so she turned left.

She could have given one of the tickets to her chauffeur. She did not even consider it. She often forgot about him. She tried to remember the colour of his eyes.

"I'm going to get more champagne," said Marianne with a pointed sigh. "Don't stay up watching the masses for too long. No one will hold The Gate for you."

"Marianne, are you sure..."

Marianne waited in the doorway, swaying slightly, a frown just barely turning the corners of her lips.

"Am I sure about what?" she asked.

Louisa shook her head.

"I don't know."

Marianne stepped towards her, using the backs of chairs and the tops of side tables for balance as she made her way. Her steps may have been unsteady, but the hand that gripped Louisa's shoulder was firm.

"I am sure," she said, smiling encouragement. "I'm sure that I want a life with you, and we aren't going to get that here. No one is. And you won't change anything staying behind. You'll just burn up with the rest of it."

"You're right," said Louisa.

"And you're going to love the 1920s," said Marianne. "It was the best decade! I'm getting more champagne. Promise you won't be late."

"I promise."

Marianne kissed her, gently, and it was sweeter than it had any right to be. Louisa watched her girlfriend as she walked away, the short flapper dress riding high up her thighs, the feathered headband endearingly askew. Marianne only half shut the study door behind her, limbs too relaxed to force it closed.

Louisa's own black dress was not time-period appropriate, but Marianne did not complain, for once. There would be an infinite number of dresses to pick from when they went back to Marianne's favourite point in history. Louisa did not mention how the '20s led to the stock market crash that led to the Great Depression, that led to a million other points that led to this moment once more. There was no point. Marianne was determined, and so excited, to go back to the '20s. She did not need to know that Louisa would not be going there with her.

The old man who sat behind the surprisingly pedestrian computer set up on a similarly simple desk near the front door of Addleburg's mansion raised an eyebrow when Louisa gave him her chosen year, but thankfully, did not comment. Marianne had already run ahead after choosing 1921, desperate for some alcohol to dampen the fear and sorrow she claimed she did not feel. Louisa expected the man to make some sort of protest, but as she thought of those roaring and doomed '20s, she supposed every year that these lucky travellers selected had some sort of drawback. Louisa's choice was no more worthy of protest than anyone else's. She did check to make sure that the man had written it down correctly, and he politely let her peer at the computer screen to ensure her wish would be granted.

She only caught a glimpse of a small portion of the list, perhaps fifty people's names at most, and was surprised by the wide variety of dates. 1955, far too close to the present end for Louisa's liking. 1599, perhaps someone wanted to see an original Shakespeare production. 1776, a historic year indeed, though Louisa imagined the traveller was not thinking about smallpox.

The man turned the screen away before she could read much more, but she had seen enough. She had confirmed her own year. She nodded at him, and presented her hand to him, one fingertip stretched outwards, waiting. The hand that grabbed her own was gentle. The prick that extracted a sample of her blood was not. But it was necessary. The Gate would locate her and send her where she wanted to go.

Standing in the study, she could still feel her heartbeat in her fingertip. It comforted her. The beat was strong. The beat was steady. At least her heart was as sure as Marianne, even if her mind still fluttered with uncertainty.

The door to the study swung open with a slight creak, and Louisa turned, expecting to see Marianne, perhaps insisting now that she join her for champagne. But an unfamiliar man stood in the doorway who looked as shocked as Louisa felt.

"Excuse me, I didn't know someone was still in here," he said. "Almost everyone has gone downstairs."

"We have five minutes," said Louisa, defensive, unsure if the man was accusing her of something, but he blushed like he was the one in the wrong.

"I know," he said.

"Oh."

The man did not seem very old, no more than ten years older than Louisa's own twenty-seven, but his short-cropped beard was already speckled with silver. He held a top hat in slightly trembling hands, and his smart suit had too many layers for Louisa to count. He looked like he stepped out of some movie about Dracula, or Frankenstein, and she supposed he was headed for the Victorian Era. She was ashamed to realize she could not think of the exact dates.

The man stepped forward, not very close to her, just closer to the screen.

"I heard the celebration and had to see," he said, though his eyes kept flitting away from Times Square to his shoes. "I used to watch every year. It seemed wrong to ignore it."

"I understand," said Louisa. "We'd always watch, too. Me and my parents. They're not here. I don't know why I told you that."

"I'm sorry."

"It's alright. I'm here with my girlfriend. We're going back to the '20s. We're going to party like Gatsby."

"That sounds like fun," said the man, though his voice was flat. "They look like they're having fun, in New York. I can't understand why. If I was there, I'd be crying. I'd be crying so hard no one could make me stop."

His face was so blank it was hard to imagine him crying, but Louisa thought he was telling the truth. It made her feel like she should, too.

"I'm not going to the '20s."

"Oh?"

"Don't tell Marianne. My girlfriend."

"Don't worry. I won't."

"Are you worried about the butterflies?" asked Louisa.

The man's eyebrow twitched, the only movement on his otherwise still blank face.

"The butterflies?"

"There was a science fiction story about it," said Louisa. "A man went into the past, killed a butterfly, and it ruined the present. With all of us going back, well, that's a lot of dead butterflies, don't you think?"

"I think the whole point of going back is that the present couldn't be any worse," said the man. "And I never liked that story. It didn't make sense to me."

"Why not?"

"Carbon dioxide."

Louisa did not understand, but the man did not elaborate. A reporter smiled as she interviewed a couple who held each other so tightly Louisa was surprised either of them had the breath to respond.

"There's only two minutes left," said Louisa. "We should go down, if we're going to make it."

The man nodded, but he did not join her as she left the study and walked down the great staircase.

She followed the sounds of forced laughter to the great hall where Lord Addleburg was giving a toast to the New Year. To the last New Year. His clothing looked like wrapped sheets, and some artificial leaves formed a crown of sorts on the top of his head. He was going way back, but even Rome fell. Louisa wanted to yell at him that Rome fell, the pain would always come, the end would always loom ahead of them, but she snapped her jaw shut and stared at the pattern beneath her feet.

The hall had been converted into a transport station, and the metal floor hummed with a promise of something great, and hopeful, and terrible. There was a pattern of light that wound in circular swirls and interlaced with geometric formations. Louisa was not sure if that was necessary for the technology or just aesthetic. It reminded her of a mandala she saw on a documentary, one made of sand by Buddhist monks. After they completed the work, a beautiful design of white and yellow and pale pink, they swept it away. The point of making it was to see it destroyed. When she was a little girl, Louisa destroyed a sandcastle she made on the beach when she saw her cousin running towards her, intent on destroying it himself. She did not make it to be destroyed, but if that was the castle's fate, she wanted to be the one to destroy it. Her eyes traced the patterns of Addleburg's mandala, so beautiful, and destined to burn with the rest of the world.

Everyone in the hall was chanting. It was a familiar chant. Louisa wondered if it was from that same documentary, some meditative prayer uttered by those monks. But it was much more familiar than that. They were counting down. They had begun the countdown to the end of the world.

When they reached seven, Louisa looked over her shoulder, but the man in the many-layered suit had not come down the steps, and she guessed he had decided to stay and celebrate with the distant, unlucky mass in Times Square.

When they reached five, she thought of her parents, and how they laughed when they found her vomiting into the toilet when she was ten years old and had stolen glass after glass of champagne.

When they reached three, she locked eyes with Marianne, and Louisa was sure that her girlfriend knew that she would find herself alone in 1921.

When they reached zero the world became unbearably bright.

And then Louisa was somewhere new.

One million years into the future.

She wanted to bear witness to the world they had destroyed with their selfishness, crushing humanity in one final blast, and leaving the earth scorched and doomed to eternal loneliness. Someone had to carry the memory of life with them, to see the pain of a barren planet that might have had a chance to continue living if Lord Addleburg and all his rich ticketholders had not decided their wealth gave them the right to determine *the end*. She was planning to look on the wasteland and remember her parents, Marianne, the man in the many-layered suit. She would be a prophet of the past in the dead, empty future.

But the future was neither empty nor dead.

Lord Addleburg's mansion was gone, but she was still surrounded by people, a massive crowd in a courtyard-like space encircled by spiralling structures that blinked in a confetti colour whirling of lights. It was like Times Square, though it was nothing like the world she knew. And the people around her were like people, though nothing like the human she was herself. Their arms were wrong, their faces and bodies, their shouting voices musical but dissonant in their unfamiliarity, just as wrong to her senses as the buildings designed to swirl in place, defying physics.

She could almost believe that the bombs had not gone off, or that the diaspora of the rich had changed the course of history, but she knew neither of those to be true. The rich had fled. The world had been destroyed. But not forever. Not completely.

What narcissism led them to believe that they had the power to end the future forever? A worldwide explosion could not stop the beginning of a new millennia any more than the flap of a butterfly wing. The world moved on, heedless of the manipulations of the self-important. Time continued, unyielding to the tantrums of creatures that would have disappeared without Lord Addleburg's help.

Louisa wanted to laugh, but the moment she breathed in to do so, she began to choke.

A few of the people in the crowd noticed her distress. Hand-like appendages tried to support her as she fell back, gasping as she suffocated on air that was nothing like her air. They called out in less musical tones, not in any language Louisa knew, but it was clear they were calling for help. The crowd around them was too loud for their pleas to be heard. Black spots began to dance in front of Louisa's eyes as her chest tightened and burned. *Carbon dioxide*, the man with the silver-speckled beard had said. The protagonist in that old science fiction story would have choked on an atmosphere so unlike his own if he had gone back in time to crush that butterfly. Now Louisa was one million years into the future, her body rejected by an atmosphere that had evolved past her ability to live in it.

She knew she should be scared, but it was hard to be scared when the crowd around her pulsed with joy. Someone cradled her head, someone whispered soothing murmurs, but she did not need to be soothed. She was one million years into the future, and there were still people in the world to celebrate, and such a reason to celebrate! One million years to the day that she disappeared from Lord Addleburg's party. If she could have spoken, if they could have understood, she would have told those kind strangers to leave her, to leave the past behind, and join the celebrations, to cheer, and sing, and welcome in the New Year.

Alexandra Grunberg is a Glasgow based author, poet, screenwriter, and artist. Her fiction has appeared in Daily Science Fiction, Cast of Wonders, and Flash Fiction Online. Learn more at her website, alexandragrunberg.weebly.com

Girl's Best Friend
Tova Hope-Liel

The first time Julia fed the monster under her bed she was five years old. Her mother was trying to convince her to place her special treat for tomorrow on her nightstand. Julia wouldn't put the chocolate bar down.

"Julia..." her mother warned. Julia clutched the chocolate bar harder.

"You said I could sleep with it!"

"Yes, but not in your bed. Just put it on the table."

"But what if the monster eats it in the middle of the night?"

"What monster?"

"The monster under my bed." Julia could hear it burble under there.

Her mother sighed in a way that Julia knew only too well. "Julia, there's no monster under your bed."

"Is too! I can hear it!"

Her mother bent down and looked under her bed. "Nothing there."

"Check again!"

Gurgle, gurgle, gurgle.

"Here, Julia. Come here."

"What if it eats me?"

"He won't eat you, honey, and even if he tries, I'll protect you. That's what mommies do."

Julia slid out of her bed slowly, skeptical of her mother's flippancy. When Julia's feet hit the ground the monster burbled again and Julia screamed, jumping behind her mother. Mommy bent down and Julia mimicked her. Mommy turned on her phone's flashlight and shined it under the bed.

Julia swallowed thickly. There was nothing there. That meant that the monster could turn invisible. That only made them scarier. Julia's knuckles turned white against her chocolate bar.

"See? Nothing there."

"But I *heard* it!" Julia insisted.

"That was just the old house creaking." Her mother said. But it didn't sound like the house. Her mother sighed. "Do you want me to bring back in your nightlight?"

"No!" Julia cried. "I'm a big girl!"

"I know you are. Listen, even if there is a monster under your bed, monsters hate the feel of blankets, so just keep your whole body under the covers and you won't have any worries. Okay?"

Julia didn't believe her.

"Can I please have the chocolate bar?" Mommy gave Julia a hard look that made her question less of one. Julia handed the chocolate over with a pout that her mother ignored. She put the chocolate bar on the bedside table. "Now remember, I don't want to see that you've eaten any in the middle of the night-"

"Mommy! I know!"

"Just reminding you," her mother said mildly. She pressed a kiss to Julia's forehead. "Goodnight, honey."

"Goodnight, Mommy."

Her mother closed the door on her way out. Julia rolled over under her covers in the dark of the room. The monster below her made a loud sound, like Julia's belly did when she was hungry. The monster must have been hungry, too.

"Hey, Monster. Can you hear me?"

Gurgle, burble, gurgle.

"My name is Julia," she whispered. "Please don't eat me."

The monster made an unconvinced gurgling noise. "Here," inspiration struck. "How about this? I'll give you some of my chocolate instead! Chocolate tastes better than children anyway."

The monster still didn't seem convinced. It burbled and its belly growled again.

"If I give you this chocolate, do you promise not to eat me?"

The monster was quiet for a moment. There was a belch that sounded a lot like a yes.

Julia scrambled up to reach her nightstand, keeping her feet under the blankets all the while. She fumbled around in the dark before finding her chocolate bar. Julia held out her other hand blindly by the edge of the bed.

"We shake on it. A real deal is always sealed with a handshake or a pinky promise. But I don't think you have a pinky, so, handshake."

The monster made a noise, as if to say that it didn't have a hand either, but Julia didn't care. There was a splorch as it unstuck whatever type of hand it had from the floor and Julia felt a thin tentacle take hers. She gave it one good shake.

"There." She carefully unwrapped the crinkly wrapper and broke off a row of pieces with a snap. Her lunch for tomorrow at school would suffer, but if she was alive by morning it would be worth it. She placed it on the ground and heard a swoop as the monster accepted her offering.

There was a contented belch.

"Good, huh?" Julia rewrapped her candy and placed it back on the nightstand. Another belch.

Julia settled into bed, making sure both of her feet were under the blanket, just in case.

Julia got in trouble the next morning. Her mother didn't believe that Julia had fed the chocolate to her monster, but Julia didn't mind much that she couldn't watch TV for the next few days. She was alive and all it had taken was a little bit of chocolate. A small price.

The next night she was almost asleep when she felt something poke her arm, which hung over the side of the bed.

Julia blinked the sleep-gunk from her eyes and scowled. "What...?"

Another poke.

The monster. Fear was like bricks in Julia's belly. The tentacle poked her a third time.

"What do you want?"

Grr-owl!

Julia's blood ran cold. It was hungry.

"I... I don't have any more chocolate."

The monster made another noise that sounded more like a growl than the one before had. Then she felt it. The tentacle brushed against her leg, patting up it like it was looking for her.

Julia screamed and pulled her leg back under the covers. She felt the tentacle press at the blanket which hung where her leg had been. The monster made a squelching noise and the pressure of its tentacle withdrew sharply.

"Julia? Julia? Are you okay?" Julia heard Daddy ask from the other side of the door.

Julia was about to scream for him to come in when she remembered that the monster was invisible. Her mother hadn't seen it, her father wouldn't either.

"I-I'm fine! Just fell off the bed!"

"Okay, sweetie. Good night."

"Night!"

The monster's belly growled again. Julia huddled under her covers. Her parents couldn't do anything. They couldn't see or hear it, and she had no more chocolate! It was going to eat her! Julia squeezed her eyes shut, listening to the burble and gurgle and growl of a hungry monster.

Julia bit her lip. She couldn't cry. Big girls didn't cry. Big girls solved their own problems. If the monster wanted candies, then candies Julia would get for it. She knew where some were. Mommy kept a stash in the cabinets above the fridge that she thought Julia didn't know about.

"Hey, can you hear me?" Julia asked the monster.

The monster belched.

"Okay… I don't have any chocolate here…" The monster's belly growled again. "But, I know where some is. If-if you let me go… I can get it. Okay? Chocolate's much better than children, remember?"

There was a silence and then the monster belched again. Julia heard its tentacles slither across the floor. She closed her eyes and hoped that the monster wouldn't eat her as she stepped off the bed. Her foot touched the ground unharmed. Julia lowered the other one, and waited.

Nothing. Julia let out a breath of relief.

Something slimy brushed against her leg and she yelped, dancing back. Julia pinwheeled backward over her bed but didn't fall like she expected. A line of wet suckers pulsed against her back — catching her.

Julia steadied herself and the tentacle dropped away. She took a step forward as quietly as she could. The floorboards creaked under her weight but otherwise she heard no sound. The monster stayed where it was.

Julia tiptoed past her parents' room and down to the kitchen, pausing whenever she heard the house settle.

Now to get the candy. Julia bit her nails. Truly, the best way was to climb up onto the counter and then onto the refrigerator to reach the cabinet above. But then she would have to either stand on the microwave which blocked her way or move it. Julia wasn't sure she was strong enough to move it. She'd just have to be quick so her foot didn't go through it like they did on TV.

Julia carefully picked up a stool next to the kitchen island. She placed it next to the counter and climbed up. There was only room for her there if she stood on her tiptoes. She eyeballed the candy cabinet and put one tentative foot on the microwave. The microwave held. Julia pushed her weight down. All seemed okay. Julia took a deep breath and hopped up. There was a terrifying popping noise but other than that the microwave seemed fine. There was no foot shaped hole in it.

Julia levered herself onto the fridge and sat, legs curled under her. She opened the cabinet, careful not to fall backwards.

There was the candy. Lollipops and cookies and chocolate bars and taffies. A kid's dream. Julia took two. One for herself — a cotton candy lollipop — and one for her monster — a strawberry taffy. Mommy didn't have any small chocolates and any bars would be noticed if they went missing.

Julia wiggled off of the fridge, dropped down to the counter, and onto the floor. She winced as her feet hit and a shock ran up her legs. *Don't cry*, she told herself sternly. *You can't wake up Mommy*. Julia closed her eyes, and whimpered for a minute. Moping for a bit always helped. Then it was time to move on, so she uncurled herself and tiptoed back upstairs.

When she opened the door to her room, the gurgling of the monster was louder. Julia bent down and placed the taffy offering under her bed. "Here. I couldn't get chocolate, but taffy is good too."

The monster belched in agreement and a tentacle lashed out, making Julia scramble back. Blood pounded in her ears. She watched it scoop up the taffy and heard a gulp. The monster stopped its burbling and Julia waited to see if it would move again, but there were no further flickers of shadow under the bed.

Eventually, Julia climbed back under her covers and placed the stolen lollipop under her pillow for safe keeping. She closed her eyes and listened hard, but the house was silent and the monster sated, it seemed.

Julia fell asleep.

The next night Julia brought the monster its food without a reminder. During dinner she'd stolen some off of her plate that she hadn't wanted to eat and hid it in a napkin. She slid out of bed after her parents went to sleep, and pulled it out.

The monster sent out a fumbling tentacle, patting the floor for its dinner. It found the napkin and poked it open. Julia watched intently. The monster sent out a second curious tentacle. Their tips rolled over the food, spreading mashed potatoes all over the napkin, reveling in the texture. The monster pulled its tentacles back under the bed and it let out a satisfied gurgle.

Julia watched as it ate her leftovers from dinner, everything except the brussels sprouts, which it spat out and placed neatly back on the napkin. It pushed the discarded food back towards Julia.

Julia curled the napkin up in her hand and stuffed it in the trash in her room. She climbed into bed and heard the monster make a humming sound. It was deep, like the sound of a vacuum. It gurgled, as if complaining about the dinner.

"Yeah," Julia agreed, "I don't like brussels sprouts either." Julia closed her eyes and curled up in her blanket.

The monster hummed again.

Julia was six when she lost her first tooth. She finished giving her monster its dinner (today it ate half a hot dog and the remains of a lollipop filled with bubblegum, since the bubblegum parts were never worth it) and she showed it the tooth.

She placed the tooth on the ground in the little plastic treasure chest her teacher had given her to keep it safe.

"It's my first," Julia said proudly.

The monster's questing tentacles poked at it and retreated suddenly.

"It's not scary. Us humans have them in our mouths. It's how we eat!"

The monster poked at it again. Gently the tentacles pulled it out of the box, probing it curiously. *Burble, gurgle.*

"Just don't break it, okay? Mommy says I need to put it under my bed for the Tooth Fairy."

It growled at her.

Julia huffed and rolled her eyes. "I know the Tooth Fairy isn't real, but Mommy wants me to anyway. I think she still believes." Only monsters were real. Fairies weren't.

The monster placed the tooth back in the treasure chest and Julia closed it. She climbed into bed and stuck it under her pillow.

"Good night, Monster."

The monster hummed back. Julia fell asleep, so used to the small sounds that the monster made she didn't even stir when it made a small burp, nor did she hear its prey's cut-off scream.

At breakfast the next morning Julia told her mother that the Tooth Fairy hadn't come. She saw the quick mouthed conversation between her parents as they each claimed that the other was supposed to switch out her tooth for money. Julia knew that the Tooth Fairy wasn't real.

"It's okay," Julia said. "Maybe tomorrow." It made her parents happy.

Julia went to school vindicated, so she wasn't at home when her father began cleaning her room and ran a broom under her bed to find four large ovular bug wings (they really needed to get better bug killer, clearly they were getting fed well enough with that dusty pink coloring) and some small glass bones. Her father didn't recognize the toys but honestly Julia had so many he didn't expect to. Though how they got under there, he had no idea.

Julia skipped right up to her room, and planted herself down on the floor next to her bed. "I figured out a name for you."

The monster made no sound of acknowledgment but Julia knew that it had heard her.

"Insquidious!"

There was a twitch as a tentacle flickered toward her.

"See, because you have tentacles like a squid and 'cuz we learned that word today in class and it means," Julia closed her eyes, trying to remember the exact words her teacher had used, "*cunning*. You know, like smart and evil. I don't think you're very evil, but you do eat children, so maybe you're a little bit evil. But I know you're smart, so I think it works. What do you think?"

Insquidious belched. A tentacle tapped on Julia's leg. Julia rolled her eyes and pulled out her stolen napkin. She placed it in front of the bed and Insquidious gobbled up the food in one gulp.

"I knew you'd like it. Gotta go brush my teeth!" Julia hopped back to her feet and skipped out.

Julia was seven when she spent her first night away from home. It was Shantelle's birthday. She was having a sleepover party, and there was no way that Julia was going to miss it.

She gave Insquidious a packet of Oreos to tide him over and she headed over to Shantelle's.

The night was amazing. Julia and her friends had so much fun. They painted each others' nails. They made s'mores in Shantelle's backyard. They gorged themselves on candy and talked about which teachers they hated. They played classic sleepover games: Bloody Mary, Light as a Feather/Stiff as a Board, and Truth or Dare.

On Shantelle's turn Jin gave her a truth: what was her deepest fear?

"Nothing. I mean, I used to be afraid of the dark. I had a nightlight and everything, but I don't need it anymore. I got rid of it a few weeks ago."

"But what about the monsters?" Julia asked.

Everyone looked at her strangely. "You still believe in that?" Jin snorted.

Quinn laughed. "Yeah, Julia, monsters aren't real."

"I-I know that!" Julia lied. "Of course. I-Of course."

"Anyway, Eliana's turn," Laquisha said, turning away.

After a while the girls started mattress surfing and Julia snuck off under the guise of grabbing fuzzy socks.

Julia turned off the lights to Shantelle's room and knelt down.

"Hey there."

The monster under Shantelle's bed hissed.

"Stop that. Now listen, I know Shantelle just got rid of her nightlight, but don't you dare eat my friend. Got it?"

The monster snarled and Julia jumped back as she heard a talon scratch against the floor. Julia scowled at it.

"No!" Julia snapped, stamping her foot at it. The talon scratched back towards the bed.

"Here. An exchange. You listening?" The monster made no noise. "This is a marshmallow." Julia placed it on the floor right next to the bed. "Try it."

The monster growled.

"Trust me. It's better than children. Marshmallows always are."

The monster growled again.

"Don't yuck something you've never even tried! Try it!"

The talon scratched back out, dragging on the ground. She heard it squish into the marshmallow and then a loud chewing noise. The monster chirped.

"Good, huh?"

The monster chirped again.

"You know, there's a whole factory where they make this stuff."

The monster made a hungry sound, like Insquidious used to.

"Take all your friends there, I'll tell you the address of one on one condition."

The monster hissed.

"You never touch a child ever again. Do I have a deal?"

There was a silence. Then, a chirp.

"Good." Julia got out her phone and looked up the closest marshmallow factory. She heard Shantelle's monster scuttle backwards under the bed, probably in fear of the light from the phone. She told the monster the address.

Laquisha jogged into the room and Julia jumped back from the bed as Laquisha turned on the light. "There you are, Julia! Come on, we're prank calling Eddie! Hurry up!"

"Coming!" Julia said, and dashed back out.

The next morning, Shantelle wasn't dead despite her lack of nightlight, so Julia figured she'd done alright.

The first time Julia didn't feed her monster, she was eight years old and she'd been kidnapped.

"Shut up, you stupid kid!" the kidnapper hissed. He kicked her in the belly and Julia couldn't help the tears that spilled forth.

Julia was a big girl. Big girls didn't cry, but the tears still streamed down her cheeks. Julia hugged her knees to her chest. Her wrists and ankles were killing her.

"Gag her," the other said and he waved a hand flippantly. There were two: one in the driver's seat and one in the back with Julia.

"No!" Julia kicked at the man near her hands, but couldn't stop him. He cuffed her on the side of the head.

Julia was going to die. She was going to die and never see her parents again and everything was going to end and-

"This is why I don't work with kids," the one near her snarled, as if Julia's age and state of being kidnapped were her own fault. Not that Julia would say any of that, even if she could speak. The man looked so scary and angry. She didn't want him to hit her again. Julia whimpered and flinched. The man kicked at her halfheartedly and missed. "Shut up."

"You want a payout, don't you?" the driver asked. The kidnapper in the back grunted. "Well, ransom works every time."

Julia had heard of ransom. She'd snuck a few episodes of that police show Mommy loved so much when she was supposed to be sleeping. Insquidious liked them too. Every time a bad guy had showed up it had made squishing noises.

Insquidious. She was never going to see it again. A fresh wave of tears filled Julia's eyes. The man next to her groaned. "Pull up here." The van stopped outside a warehouse. The man next to her grabbed her by the waist of her pants and carried her out of the van. Julia wiggled and cried but that only earned her a mean pinch. "Stop that!"

Julia wanted to cry again, but no tears came. She'd cried herself dry. They walked into the warehouse where a bearded man greeted them cheerfully. "Go well?"

"Easy peasy," the driver said.

The man who held Julia put her in a chair and held her down. She tried to wiggle and fight against him, but with her arms and feet bound there was little she could do. The kidnapper took out the roll of duct tape he'd used to bind her legs and arms originally as well as an Exact-O knife from a pocket in his pants. He cut the binds open for a second so he could tape her arms and legs to the limbs of the chair.

He walked over to his friends who sat at a table with a computer. The rest of the warehouse was empty and echoed. The only lights that were turned on were the ones over Julia and the ones over their work-station. Julia struggled again. She screamed wordlessly, until the man who hated kids threatened to carve her up. Julia shut her mouth with a whimper.

The police would come for her. Her parents would. Someone had to. She couldn't die here! She couldn't-! Keep calm, Julia. You're going to be okay. Kids were always saved on TV. It was scary and it took the police until the last second but they were always saved.

Right?

"Okay, kid," Bearded Man said. "Can you read? Nod for yes."

Julia nodded. She was eight year old! Of course, she could read!

"Good. Meanie, cut her gag off and get the camera." Bearded Man told the man with the knife. Meanie grunted but did. Julia worked her jaw—it was sore from the gag. Meanie pulled out a handheld camera. "Kook. You got the cards?" The driver—Kook—held up giant cards with words printed on them.

They were so calm, Julia thought numbly. How could they be so calm about this? They'd kidnapped someone! Clearly they did this a lot, and got away with it. Otherwise, wouldn't they have been scared of the cops?

"Okay kid: action!" Bearded Man said.

A red light lit the camera. Kook pointed to the signs, dimly illuminated by the warehouse lights. "My name is-your name here?"

The recording stopped. "Don't mess around kid, you know what you were supposed to say!" Meanie snarled. Julia winced. "Mess up again, I'll make you wish you hadn't."

Neither Bearded Man nor Kook looked concerned. "Try again," Bearded Man said. His fingers clicked along the keyboard. "And... action."

"My name is Julia Johnson. I am okay. But if you do not give these men-"

"Read the sign correctly!" Meanie shouted, taking out his knife.

Julia burst into tears. Kook rolled his eyes. "Meanie, calm down. We don't want her bleeding just yet. Good faith and all that."

Meanie narrowed his eyes at her behind the ski mask he wore.

"Sorry," Kook told her, "he's new. Clearly. Now, let's try this again. Okay?"

Julia managed to nod, still crying. But she read all the signs just the way the men holding her wanted her to. The Bearded Man grinned. "Perfect. The crying adds another element of intensity to the video. And... sending... now."

"Well boys, now we just wait for the pay-day. Who's up to lose some of their future money?" Kook pulled out a pack of cards. Julia calmed herself down, hiccuping quietly.

"Oo! Me!" Bearded Man said.

"I have to pee!" Julia shouted.

"Don't care," Kook said. The others ignored her. Julia didn't really need to pee, but now she was worried for when she did have to.

Julia squirmed some more, but she couldn't pull free of the duct tape and every wiggle hurt as the tape pulled at her skin.

"If you stay still and your parents cooperate, there's no need for you to get hurt. Okay, kid?" Bearded Man called. Julia froze in her struggles. His eyes were cold through the mask. Julia wanted to just disappear. She wanted her parents. She wanted to just go home.

Julia waited for so long that she was sure days and days must have passed, except that the men didn't seem to be eating much. They'd drink beer, play cards, leave to go to the bathroom, and watch scary movies on their computer. Julia closed her eyes. Maybe time would go faster if she was asleep, and she was starting to need to pee. If she fell asleep her body would stop her from peeing, she was sure. She never wet her bed anymore anyway, so why would this be any different? Plus, she was exhausted. It must have been way past her bedtime.

Julia leaned her head back against the chair. Accustomed to blocking out Insquidious' idle noises, she drifted in and out of sleep, ignoring the sounds from the action movie they watched. There was a loud bang, and Julia whimpered and tried to shift into a more comfortable position. Their movie was really loud. She wished they'd turn it down.

"What the shit?"

"What is wrong with you, Mark-?"

Julia opened her eyes. Mark. So one of their names was Mark.

"I saw something!"

"What do you mean, something? Did you see a big bad bug?"

Mark—Kook—rolled his eyes. His head turned this way and that, looking for whatever it was. "No, something… never mind. Doesn't matter." He turned back to the movie. So that gunshot had been real? Kook had done that? That wasn't the movie? Julia shivered.

"Fine, but no more shooting. That scared the shit out of me," Bearded Man grumbled. They were about to turn the movie back on when Meanie's chair was yanked out from under him.

Julia's jaw dropped. The chair was thrown against the wall and it shattered—pieces scattering everywhere. Julia jumped at the

noise, duct tape pulling on her limbs painfully. What…?

Meanie jumped to his feet, knife out. The other two joined him, glancing about nervously.

"I didn't just hallucinate that, did I?" Meanie asked.

Kook's gun was out, he was breathing heavily. "Don't think so…"

They were terrified. Julia scowled at them. *Good.*

Every light bulb in the room exploded. Julia closed her eyes and felt small shards of glass rain down on her hair. She shook them out. When she opened her eyes again, she couldn't see anything.

The gun went off. The kidnappers began screaming.

Someone had come to save her.

Julia felt… she wasn't even sure. Her heart was beating fast and she had a steady pounding in her ears. Her breath was coming quickly. Her chest felt like it was bubbling. She bit down on her tongue so as not to let out the giggles that filled her belly.

She was safe.

She was *saved.*

"There! I heard something!" A flurry of gunshots echoed through the warehouse. Julia winced, eyes closed. If they couldn't see, they might hit her! How could she stop that-?

Someone screamed and there was a loud growl. The scream ended and Julia heard a gulp.

"Over there!"

"Meanie?"

"Kook!"

"Blackbeard! It got Black-" A loud *BANG! Gulp.*

"Kook!" The growling got louder. "No…" Meanie cried. "Please … please I'm begging you, don't hurt me, please-!"

But the thing in the dark didn't care. It swallowed Meanie too.

Julia could hear it move across the floor, dragging across the dirty ground. What if this invisible monster hadn't come to help her?

What if it was going to kill all of them? Julia whimpered. It squelched as it got closer. It stopped right before her, and Julia could feel it snuffling just millimeters from her face.

And gurgling.

"In-Insquidious?" Julia asked hopefully. Her voice caught.

Something damp dragged up her arm and up to her face. It brushed a tentacle over her cheek which was still wet from when she'd cried. It made a deep growl. Julia let out a gasp of relief.

Insquidious. It had come for her.

Julia was crying again. Insquidious wiped the tears away gently. "You came."

Insquidious made an offended noise. She felt the duct tape bonds ripped away and she yelped, clenching one of its tentacles in her hands. With the tape gone, Julia jumped at Insquidious, hugging it. She'd never hugged Insquidious before, nor touched it much. But now, she felt like she'd never let go. It was furry on the back, wet and filled with pulsing suckers on its belly. It was also huge in a way that made Julia wonder how it managed to fit under her bed. It was probably fat from all the candy. Insquidious didn't touch her back at first. Hesitantly, its tentacles wrapped around her, as if it wasn't sure how to hug. Julia tightened her grip to show it, and it mimicked her.

"I'm so happy you came."

Gurgle, burble.

"I know," Julia laughed, "I know. You haven't eaten. I bet candy tastes better than bad guys, too."

Insquidious made a retching noise that made Julia laugh again. She stroked one of its tentacles fondly. The damp touch and regular pulsing of the suckers felt like waves on the shore to her, almost as if Insquidious was rocking her to sleep. Julia's eyes fluttered closed. Tonight had been really exhausting. Insquidious gurgled, belly trembling beneath her.

"I missed you too," Julia whispered. "Let's go home, okay?"

Insquidious began the slow lurch home, and Julia held it tightly.

"I must owe you a whole chocolate bar for this, huh?"

Insquidious held Julia closer and belched in agreement.

This is the second of Tova's stories we've published – Palingenesis is available now for free on our website, We predict a long and promising writing career ahead. She can usually be found reading or writing, and though she loves to swim she still can't shapeshift into a mermaid, much to her dismay.

Subscribe!

Get the latest issues direct your door as soon as the ink is dry, Science fiction, fantasy and a hint of mayhem from deepest space to your darkest thoughts. *Wyldblood Magazine* – every two months.

Six issues only **£35/$49** (print) or **£15/$21** (digital) from us or single issues from us and Amazon worldwide (£5.99/$7.99 print, £2.99/3.99 digital).

The Portal

Matias Travieso-Diaz

So far, the crowning point of my career as a Middle Eastern Studies scholar had been the release by Screeching Owl, Ltd. of my treatise, *"The Great Old Ones and Others – The Lost History of the Ancient Deities."*

Screeching Owl was reluctant to take on publishing a six-hundred-page tome on the stories and myths surrounding the powerful deities from space that once ruled the Earth and have since fallen into a deep sleep. "There is no market for that kind of crap," an editor proclaimed.

I was able to convince him and others at the firm that there *is* a market for this esoteric area of scholarship by citing novels, movies, short stories, and even Ph.D. dissertations dealing with the topic. I told them a good number of people dread the possibility that ancient monsters might just be waiting for a chance to return to reclaim the planet. In short, I overwhelmed their opposition with facts, figures and sales projections.

I was soon proved right: announcement of the impending release of my book in the trade press was followed by a healthy number of pre-publication orders; four months later, Amazon sales upon release of the work exceeded even the rosiest predictions of the publishers.

2

At the end of the quarter, I was awaiting my first royalty payment. Since Screeching Owl was headquartered in London and I lived in rural New Mexico, payments would occur via SurePay, a multi-national company operating an online payments system that handles money transfers between consumers and merchants, and among business entities. Use of a middleman like SurePay was far more convenient and secure than payment by check or other forms of money exchange.

Thus, in the afternoon of last December 31, I received notice that a royalty payment of $1,753.88 had come from Screeching Owl, and was told that I should sign onto my SurePay account to claim it. I became very excited, beaming with pride at my wife: "My first royalties from the book on the Old Gods have arrived!" She had been skeptical of the economic value of my research and writing of the book, so the money would also settle in my favor this dispute between us. But, more importantly, I could really use the money. I was a non-tenured college professor who specialized in an obscure branch of learning. Even in a remote corner of a less than prosperous state, life was expensive and we lived hand to mouth, like many Americans do these days. My mortgage payment was due in a week.

So, I checked onto my SurePay account, looking for the money that I would immediately direct to my bank account in Las Cruces. The money was not there. I tried multiple times over the course of the day, to no avail.

Because of the time difference, it was already New Year's Day in London, and all businesses were closed. I could not get hold of anybody, and was not about to pester my editor in the middle of the night; there was nothing she could do, in any case.

It was nine hours earlier in New Mexico than in London, but midnight was also approaching here. While everyone else was drinking and partying, I spent the last hours of the year trying to figure out how to get hold of my money.

3

When I signed into my SurePay account online, I was offered three help choices: go to the resolution center; ask for "community help;" and go to the message center and attempt to communicate by e-mail with someone. I tried all three. The advice from the "resolution center" would help only if I was disputing a transaction; here there was no transaction and nothing to dispute. The "community help" recommendation was to suggest that if I had not received an amount due because of a mistake, I should correct the mistake and try again; this I could not do, because I was not sure there was a mistake and, in any event, it was not my error but someone else's. Finally, the message center just raised all kinds of potential issues and offered suggested solutions. I kept asking to be transferred to a representative, and instead of complying, the site software kept demanding that I answer questions about my problem and suggesting inapplicable fixes. I kept calling for "customer service" and, later pleaded "human, human, human, I want to speak with a human!!" After an eternity and numerous tries, I was offered the option of sending a message describing my issue but warning that representatives would be available only during business hours and responses would be slow at times of high traffic. Thus, the first opportunity for a customer service contact would be 9 a.m. during working days. Since New Year fell on a Friday, that meant there would be nobody to help me until Monday.

Disheartened, I went to bed at 3 a.m., having missed all the New Year celebrations.

I was in a sullen mood on Saturday but contacted my editor right after I got up. She was at work and was able to look at the record of the royalty payment. "Yes, we transferred the money to your SurePay account Thursday evening, just before we closed shop."

"Let's double-check something. To what account did you direct the transfer?"

"Why, to your 'Oldgods1$@gmail.com' account."

"Oh, you must have forgotten that I had to open a new account because of the hacking incident in November. It's now 'Newgods1$@gmail.com.'"

There was an embarrassed silence on the line. Then: "Let me see if I can get that transfer cancelled or redirected to you."

"I'll keep doing the same" I promised. "First one who gets this problem solved should tell the other right away."

4

Monday went by, and then Tuesday, and Wednesday. I kept getting no response to my requests to speak to someone. The tone and content of my monologue with the computer turned more irritated and ultimately became abusive. I was on the line frequently with the editor, who was equally frustrated at her failure to connect with anyone. Finally, late Thursday evening, as I was getting ready for bed, three miraculous little dots appeared on the previously blank screen of my laptop and someone typed in: "Hello. This is Andrea. How can I help you?"

I was so shocked that I almost did not respond, but finally gathered my wits and explained: "In the transaction that I identified in earlier messages, the merchant sent me a seventeen hundred and fifty dollar payment, only it was sent to the wrong account."

"Do you know the account to which it was sent?"

"Yes."

"Do you have an e-mail account under that name?"

"No, but I can create one right away."

"Please do that. I will open a new SurePay account for you under the new name. The money will appear on that account when you sign into it."

Ten minutes later, the royalty payment was on its way to my bank.

5

A lot had happened in the intervening week. Failure of the royalty transfer had prevented me from paying two credit card balances, resulting in the imposition of late charges and a drop in my credit rating. Automatic payments to a couple of utilities and internet service providers had failed, causing my accounts to be threatened with suspension. My wife was increasingly mad at the dereliction of my head of household duties and refused to cook for us, forcing upon me the indignity of eating at fast food Mexican restaurants. I had lost sleep, my blood pressure had risen to stratospheric levels, and the lack of an outlet for my anger was surely shortening my life.

I shared my frustration with the Screeching Owl editor and she was sympathetic to my complaints but unhelpful. "That's the way the world runs these days. Anyone with power over even a small corner of the Internet can lord over you."

I was too upset to concede she had a valid point. Instead, I persisted: "I want revenge. There must be something I can do to get back at those bastards."

There was a brief silence, while I could almost hear the wheels inside her brain turning. "Well," she finally said. "Aren't you the world's leading expert on the Great Old Ones?"

"Yes, but…"

"Why don't you enlist their help in getting you satisfaction?"

It was perhaps intended as a throwaway remark, but it got me thinking.

6

Opening a portal to the realm outside time where the Old Ones are confined was not that difficult for an expert like me. Without getting into boring details, all that was needed was a supply of each of the four elements (wind was hardest to get; I had to fish out a desktop fan from the days before air conditioning); white chalk, to draw a pentagram within a large circle of the floor of the attic; many lit black candles for atmosphere; and some knowledge of Akkadian, the ancient language of Assyria and Babylon. I positioned myself outside the circle, extinguished all extraneous lights, and recited an invocation from a version of the Tablet of Destinies I had found in a Baghdad museum.

I had to try the invocation four times, more and more loudly, until a vague form of dun colored mist began to materialize in the pentagram. Even before fully forming, the presence made itself known: "Stop that racket, will ye? It's quite annoying." This, in English with a decidedly Jersey Shore accent.

I had expected to summon a vast, threatening ghost like the jinni that appeared before Aladdin in The Arabian Nights. I was ready to cower, prostrate myself, and beg for the apparition's indulgence. No need. What came out into the circle was a misshapen, gray, hairless little figure with an oversize head, small beaded eyes gleaming with malice, twisted limbs, and oversized claws. It was naked and of indeterminate sex, and seemed more pitiful than awe inspiring.

"Who… who are you?" I questioned, half in fear, but at the same time fighting to refrain from tittering.

"My name is Bingaith. I'm one of the countless spawns of Shub-Niggurath, the Mother of all."

"Are you *really* one of the Great Old Ones?" I questioned, indelicately suggesting doubt.

"You mortals are always classifying things. I'm great enough" Bingaith replied, a bit peevishly.

"O, Great One, pardon my ignorance!" I was quick to abash myself. "I summoned you to seek assistance on a grave matter."

"I'll decide whether your matter is grave and warrants my intervention. And I will set my price if I deign to help you."

I described my grievances against SurePay and my generalized anger at how modern society has made people enslave themselves to machines so they can spend more time watching stupefying tripe in front of their television sets.

Bingaith listened to my tirade without registering any reaction. However, when I ran out of steam he commented: "I'm familiar with your problems. I learned English watching *The Real Housewives of New Jersey*. I can tell you that early on, when humans were barely above the level of apes, things were simpler and people were closer to the demands of their genetic imprint. Hunting,

eating, mating and not getting killed by a predator were the main preoccupations of those of your kind. You have perverted what Nature intended for your species and gotten yourselves in all sorts of trouble. Why should I help you with your self-inflicted difficulties?"

I replied tartly: "I don't understand why you are so picky. From all I've read, those of your kind were utterly defeated in a war that took place eons ago, and are imprisoned in a frozen hell outside time and space. You linger there hoping to come back one day to rule the Earth. I have brought you back and given you a chance to open the door to the Old Ones so they can return. Why are you reluctant to venture in?"

Bingaith's response was full of undisguised contempt. "The bonds that tied us have loosened with time. We can return to this planet, as we have done to many others, any day we want, provided we are extended a proper invitation. The question is why would we want to rule a dump of a world on the verge of ruin?"

"Perhaps things are less dire than you believe. Maybe you should get a better understanding of the modern world before giving us the back of your hand."

Bingaith stared at me fixedly, exuding evil from his loathsome features. "Alright. I'll do as you ask. I'll wreak havoc on that company against which you hold a grudge. But if returning to this world is not to my liking, I'll come back to collect from you. In blood."

7

Several days went by. I awaited anxiously for news of the destruction of the SurePay headquarters that Bingaith had promised. Surely, a catastrophic event of that nature would have been all over the news media. But there was silence.

I refused to believe that even a minor Old deity would renege on his commitments. When the suspense proved too great to endure, I conducted another summoning. Again, I had to repeat the words of the incantation several times before getting a response; but, this time, what materialized in the portal was quite a different figure.

Bingaith was no longer naked, but was dressed in a three-piece pinstripe suit, with a white shirt and a silk power tie. He was outfitted with Louboutin dress shoes and wore enormous Giorgio Armani sunglasses that covered most of his hideous face. The claws had been carefully manicured and, what could be seen of his skin, appeared suntanned.

"What do you want now?" was his harsh greeting.

Trying not to sound irritated, I responded: "I was wondering when you are going to make good on the promise you made about SurePay."

Bingaith opened its mouth in a horrible imitation of a smile that displayed all his sharp teeth. "Clearly, you don't get news here in the boondocks. It was done three days ago."

"Come on, the destruction of the headquarters of a big Silicon Valley company would have been in all the newspapers."

Bingaith's attempt at a smile became even more horrible as it grew wider. "Who said I promised that the company headquarters would be destroyed? That was your idea, not mine."

"So, what did you do instead?" I almost shouted.

"Well, being from the area around Babylon and such, I had never made it to California. It is really very nice out there. I like it."

"And?"

"Here, this will explain everything to you." Bingaith produced a piece of paper from the inner pocket of his jacket and handed it to me. Its heading read: "SurePay announces reorganization, outlines plans to increase profitability." Below was a summary of a press release:

"SurePay (Nasdaq SUPY) announced last night a complete revamping of its management team and an ambitious plan to streamline its money transferring services. All members of the Board of Directors and the company's upper management have agreed to resign; each one is to receive a bonus payment in the tens of millions of dollars. In their place, a new Board and executive team have taken over the management of the multi billion-dollar company. At the helm of the new team is Rashid Ahmed Bingaith, a native of the United Arab Emirates and a graduate of the Wharton Business School.

"In a conference call with the business press, Mr. Bingaith announced plans for a drastic reduction of personnel at SurePay's offices, with the goal of making the company's services nearly 100% automated. 'The human element has been the main source of inefficiency in our operations. Our aim is to have our services provided by state-of-the art, proven software that will make monetary transfers even faster and more reliable than they are today' said Mr. Bingaith..."

I stopped reading. "What did you do to the old managers of SurePay?" I didn't really want to know, but felt compelled to ask.

"Why, we ate them" chortled Bingaith, as a viscid tongue flickered in and out his mouth. "And then we replaced them with some of my brothers, which I brought over through your portal."

I became a little nervous. "Where does that leave me?"

"You have nothing to fear. I am extending you professional courtesy. After all, it was your idea that got us involved again in human affairs. By the way, I am starting to convince others among the Old Gods that it is time for them to make their comeback to Earth, and that corporate takeover is a much better way for them to rule than through carnage."

"Does that mean that I will have to summon each Old God who wishes to re-enter our planet?"

"No. As long as the original portal remains intact, they may come and go freely without your involvement. But I have to go now. I have a company to run."

8

A week afterward, my attic had become the Grand Central Station of Old Gods traffic. The comings and goings were frequent and noisy enough that we had to cordon off the portion of the family room that lay beneath the attic and had to give up use of the entertainment center. My wife was increasingly livid; I had explained to her that I was running a delicate experiment in the attic and the commotions would soon cease, but she was not assuaged.

Then, some recently reorganized companies began attempting to acquire each other, in a series of wild proxy fights between factions of the Old Gods. I no longer dared enter the family room, since some of the raucous sounds coming out of the attic above were blood curdling.

I became tempted to move to a nearby motel for fear that the fights would spill to other parts of the house and would impact us. However, I was concerned that abandonment of the premises might cause the portal to collapse and direct the ire of the deities against us, so I did nothing. But after weeks of ceaseless turmoil, I judged that I had to do something to at least clarify our situation.

I tiptoed into the attic one mid-afternoon, usually the quietest time for otherworldly appearances. The room was eerily quiet. I started going through the invocation routine and was in the middle of my recitation from the Tablet of Destinies when there was a rush of hot air and Bingaith materialized on the pentagram.

His looks had worsened since our last encounter. He was naked, like the first time we met, and exhibited what appeared to be burn marks, missing chunks of anatomy, and other signs of physical distress.

I could not contain my amazement, and again asked an indelicate question: "Bingaith, you look like hell. What happened to you?"

Bingaith snapped its teeth in an attempt to take a bite off my body. I jumped behind a recliner and found myself apologizing again to the little monster.

"A million pardons, I didn't mean to criticize. But you are not wearing fancy clothes or designer dark glasses. I was merely noting the change."

"Mortal, watch your every word. I must come when you summon me, but that doesn't mean I have to be nice to you."

"Oh, you are always nice to me," I replied hypocritically.

"OK, stop the bull. Why have you forced me back?"

I came clean with my misgivings. "I was happy to see how you fixed my grievance with SurePay and just as glad that you took care of several other corporate malefactors. But then I have been reading accounts that suggest you guys are going at each other, and that concerns me. Where is it all going to end? And what's going to happen to us mortals?"

Bingaith seemed to be ready to jump at me again, but restrained himself:

"The Old Gods had been away from this planet for so long that we had forgotten how nice things can be around here. Earth is, for the most part, beautiful and you monkeys are easy to manipulate and control, and are tasty snacks to boot.

"I made a bad mistake. As more among us came over through the portal at my suggestion, there was increased appreciation for how pleasant life can be in this corner of creation. And that was the problem: there are too many of us and too little Earth to enjoy. Our kind doesn't like to share, we prefer to overcome others by force and consume all who challenge us.

"So, we have been fighting with each other for dominance over the world. And as is the case with the human nations, some of us are stronger than others, and after a while the weaker ones have been disposed of, and what's left are several factions of what you would call super-powers.

"Alas, the spawns of Shub-Niggurath are not the greatest of the Old Ones. We had the advantage of getting here first, but since then several of the mightiest Old Gods have come through the portal: Baoht Z'uqqa-Mogg, Cthulhu, his sister Cthaeghya, Gisguth, and others. I and my team were eliminated in the first round of the fight, but the battles among the strongest Old Ones continue."

Bingaith fell silent. I waited a bit to see if he would resume his tale, but he seemed to have run out of steam. So, I asked still another indelicate question:

"What happened to you then?"

This time Bingaith was able to get hold of my shirt and began pulling me towards him. I clung onto the arms of the recliner and fought for dear life to avoid being consumed. At length, Bingaith appeared to calm down. He let go of my shirt and continued:

"We losers are confined back in the prison outside time from which we had escaped. But now we are watched by our siblings to ensure we do not try to make a comeback."

"Does that mean that the more powerful of the Old Ones will continue to make war on each other?"

"Yes, and sometime soon they will turn against humans openly and enslave them all."

"Will we ever get relief from this plague?" It felt hopeless.

"You will get a bit of relief from us each month. The Old Ones must return to their place of captivity for one night and one day, at the rising of the full moon. We use that time to settle scores, resolve grievances, and plan future forays into other worlds."

"Every month?"

"Yeah. Like eight days from now, when the full moon returns. You will get a quiet day then. Enjoy it."

9

I agonized day and night over the Old Gods problem, and in the course of a week I developed a plan and got ready to carry it out. By the early afternoon of the day the full moon was to rise, I had bought (paying cash) a large container of chlordane, a highly flammable insecticide, at a lawn care store. I filled every corner of the attic with chlordane-soaked rags, tied to each other by a thin strip of cloth soaked with chlordane that would serve as the trigger. I did not use gasoline because chlordane is odorless, whereas the smell of gasoline could give the game away. I sprinkled the rest of the chlordane into the fireplace to increase the combustion potential.

I went to bed as usual, but did not sleep. I got up carefully, making sure not to wake up my wife, and stared in silence out of the kitchen window until the full spring moon rose into heavens.

After waiting a few minutes out of caution, I climbed the stairs to the attic and opened the door to a welcome, silent darkness. I took out a book of matches, lit a match to the strip of cloth, closed the attic door, and ran downstairs as fast as my legs would carry me.

I was out of breath when I reached the bedroom, and the breathlessness lent credibility to my voice when I screamed at my sleeping wife: "FIRE!" – "FIRE!" – THE HOUSE IS ON FIRE!!!! WE NEED TO GET OUT!!!"

We barely had time to clear the front door, half naked, as blinding flames and smoke erupted out of the attic and moved quickly through the clapboard house. We were shivering with cold and shock when the fire brigade arrived. They handed us blankets and cups of steaming coffee to get warm as we watched the firemen fight in vain to save the house from the engulfing fire.

10

The insurance company investigators had trouble reaching a conclusion as to the causes of the fire. On the one hand, they found a couple of partially consumed rags in the ruins of the attic. Those might or might not had been soaked with something, but that something had evaporated. There were also a number of strange things strewn around, including gardening soil, a large vat that had contained water, and a charred vintage fan. On the other hand, the house was not worth much and the insurance recovery would go mainly to the mortgage company. Their investigation of my affairs showed that I was a renowned scholar, in no financial trouble.

At the end, they paid off a couple of hundred thousand dollars for the house and its contents. I dickered over my share of the settlement proceeds, but pocketed the small payment that was due us. I never had thought that I would some day make money out of committing arson.

11

This all happened six months ago. In that period, I wrote a sequel to my treatise, this time a semi-fictional narrative entitled "Conversations with the Old Ones." I did not mention Bingaith by name and advanced the concept that, contrary to popular belief, the world would take a turn for the worse if the Old Ones came back to restore order. Screeching Owl literally tore the manuscript out of my hands and published it in record time. It is now number four in the New York Times non-fiction best sellers list.

My wife and I have found a new source of discord: what to do with the insurance proceeds and the royalties we are getting. We'll probably end up buying a condo in Taos, as far from our former abode as we can get without leaving New Mexico.

I would have gladly accepted the loss of all my possessions as just punishment for past misdeeds. It would have been worth it to end up penniless, just to make sure that the portal for the migration of Old Ones into this world was closed.

My contract with Screeching Owl requires that all royalty payments be made by direct bank-to-bank transfer. I reckon that banks are safe, at least for the time being. Although these days one never knows.

Matias Travieso-Diaz was born in Cuba and migrated to the United States as a young man. He became an engineer and lawyer and practiced for nearly fifty years. He retired and turned his attention to creative writing. His stories have been published or accepted for publication in about fifty paying short story anthologies, magazines, audio books and podcasts, most recently the Grantville Gazette, After Dinner Conversation, Red Room Press (YEAR'S BEST HARDCORE HORROR VOL. 6), The Copperfield Review; and The Quiet Reader. A collection of some of his stories has also been accepted for publication.

Wyld Flash

New **free** flash fiction the Wyldblood way.

Every Friday on the website.

www.wyldblood.com

Two by Two

Shawn Kobb

"Please proceed to adoption room three." The voice was robotic, but clearly intended to sound serene and unthreatening. It emanated from a small bit of plastic in the hands of a woman sitting nearby.

The family next to Jayson rose quickly, three children speaking at once, their parents attempting to shush them and herd them toward the indicated adoption room. The kids were bouncing, the excitement overwhelming their young brains.

Jayson looked down at the holographic notifier in his hands, willing it to life. He lacked the anticipation of those children, but he longed for the process to be over. If it was going to happen, he wanted it over quickly. Rip the bandage off, as his father used to say, after the fact and over Jayson's wailing.

Jayson's only consolation was that his family wasn't present. He may have lost the war, but that was one battle he had at least been victorious in.

"Fine," he had said, defeated. "We'll do it, but I'm going myself."

"But—" both of his children had started in unison.

"No *but*," Jayson had said. "I'm the one signing my name at the bottom of the contract. I'll go and I'll pick it...them out."

His children had looked ready to protest further, but before Jayson had a chance to say anything his wife had interrupted.

"Your father is right," Dian said. "While he does the adoption, we'll get the house ready. There is so much to do." She'd put on a cheerful voice and shuffled the children away, turning back to give me a wink. A neutral bystander might have seen a gesture of marital support. Jayson saw his wife declare victory.

Now, a few hours later he sat and he waited, the notification device stubbornly silent on his lap. Jayson looked over his pre-adoption documentation once more.

Please be honest in your assessment. This is for the safety and well-being of both you and your future companion lifeforms.

"Companion lifeforms," Jayson mumbled and sighed.

"Kind of dumb, I know. But don't let them catch you saying the *P* word."

He looked to the woman sitting to his right. She had her own documentation and holographic notifier in her lap. She smiled at him.

"Let me guess," she said. "Kids begged until you caved?"

Jayson nodded. "Yeah, pretty much. The wife too."

"Ouch! Double teamed. You never had a chance." She held out her hand. "I'm Amyla."

He rearranged the items on his lap to take it. "Jayson. Here alone?"

"My husband. Just ran to the toilet. Nerves, I think."

"Not his idea?"

"*Definitely* his idea," Amyla said. "He hounded me with the patriotic duty line until I caved. Don't get me wrong. He's right. We have the means. We have the space. We should probably do our part to help the cause."

"I guess," Jayson said. He looked around the sterile, white waiting room. "Isn't this why we have a government? Pay taxes? What do I know about keeping aliens as pets?"

Amyla's head whipped around quickly to make certain no one was listening. "*Companion life form*," she said quietly, but forcefully. "I'm serious. They will boot you from the program right quick if they catch you saying..." She mouthed the word *pet.*

Jayson felt a rush of heat to his cheeks. "Sorry."

"Besides," she said, forcing a smile. "You must have heard the rumors. The Ark was only the first. There were millions of xenomorphs on it. If more come, each as full?"

"Sounds more like an invasion."

She frowned. "You really need to watch what you say."

"No. I mean, you're right. I'm not saying..."

Amyla smiled again, but he felt a distance between them now. "It's okay. It's a big step. I just hope we get something..." She seemed uncertain how to end the sentence.

Jayson shrugged, but understood the sentiment. Everyone had their own horror story. If you didn't have a personal connection to someone with a terrible companion life form match, then all you had to do was go online or watch television. There was no shortage of terrible tales.

From Jayson's own office a buddy had been forced to move his family into a hotel for a week after their house burned down due to the explosive nature of the mating ritual of his newly acquired Flame-tailed Devil Lizards. Sure, the government picked up the tab as part of the adoption program, but what a hassle. Whatever Jayson ended up with, he wanted it to be as easy, safe, and clean as possible.

His cousin had received what could best be described as a pair of grapefruit-sized chunks of crystal. Supposedly, they were some sort of silicon-based life, aging at a rate a thousand times slower than humans. The rocks were so slow as to be virtually inanimate. Every few days his cousin just had to push them a few inches back so they didn't fall off his bookcase. Jayson thought that sounded perfect. Put them on the shelf, sprinkle them with a bit of sand from time to time for food. Ideal.

Jayson didn't expect he would be so lucky. It wasn't his lot in life.

"Aren't you nervous?" he asked Amyla.

She smiled. "A little, I guess. My neighbor lost all the toes on his right foot when his Silver-backed Razorcat mistook them for sausages one night."

"You see, *that's* what I'm talking about," Jayson said, his voice rising. Noting Amyla's discomfort he forced himself back to a whisper. "Doesn't that terrify you?"

"Sure, there's risks, but that's what the paperwork is for, right? They won't assign you something you can't handle. Besides, what are the alternatives?"

"Launch them back into space?" Jayson laughed after he said it, hoping to deflect, but saw Amyla's face blanch. "Just kidding."

"Right. A bit of advice? Keep your jokes to yourself when you go in there. They don't have much of a sense of humor about the program."

He nodded. She was right. As much as he wasn't interested in adding a companion life form to the family, there were government perks that he couldn't resist. His wife and kids might be focused on the chance to add a pair of aliens to the family, but Jayson had a more pragmatic approach. They needed the monthly stipend. His wife had lost her job and his salary wasn't enough. Everyone knew the companion life form allowance was exorbitantly high, more than enough to care for the creatures, clearly an incentive to nudge those like Jayson into enrolling.

"Adding a companion isn't supposed to be about money, Jayson," Dian had said. She was an idealist. "It is our duty to the human race. Plus, the kids will love it."

At first, he had thought to himself. After a few weeks the novelty would wear off and he knew who would be cleaning up giant piles of fluorescent pink alien poop in the backyard.

"I know it isn't about the money," he'd said. "But it does come with certain financial incentives. That's all I'm saying."

"Besides," Amyla was saying. "You can't really count on coming out ahead on the money. Different companions have different needs. My dentist told me he spends close to six thousand dollars a month on scrap metal just to keep his Three-headed Screaming Tunnel Birds fed."

"Six grand?" Jayson said. "That more than the entire allotment."

"That's what I'm saying. The stipend is an estimate. With millions of species, there's so much we just don't know about the xenomorphs. You can't expect to just spend a few bucks and pocket the rest. If you don't take care of your companion properly, you can go to jail."

It was bullet point three in section two of the seventy-four page adoption certificate he had signed. Jayson sighed and looked again at his paperwork and wondered if it was too late to back out. Maybe he could convince Dian and the kids that they'd been rejected.

No. He had agreed. All he could do was hope for the best. He'd kill for some of those silicon rocks like his cousin, but knew that wasn't likely. As terrible—or very rarely, great—as someone else's companion life form turned out to be, it was useless as an indicator for what you might receive. Millions of creatures, and each was different. That was the point of an ark. Every pair was presumably the last of its kind. It was an incredible responsibility. He wondered if the aliens who launched the ship ever had humanity in mind as their potential saviors?

Jayson nearly jumped out of the hard plastic chair and dropped his holographic indicator, when his neighbor's went off. A ghostly six-inch image of a smiling young woman appeared on Amyla's indicator.

"Please proceed to adoption room seven," the projected woman said, her voice serene and soothing.

"Well," Amyla said, getting to her feet. "That's us."

"What about your husband?"

"Over there." She hooked her thumb toward a drinking fountain. The man was pale and clammy. She noticed Jayson's look of concern. "Don't worry about him. He vomited the last time we bought a new car. He'll be fine."

Jayson felt he should say something. "Good luck?"

Amyla cocked her head to the side and smiled. "It'll turn out fine, Jayson. Think about the birth of your children. You didn't know what they would be like, right? And I'm sure they turned out great."

True, he thought, but Jayson had been pretty confident they weren't likely to spew acid, require a regular steady diet of petrified wood, or be invisible either.

"Yeah," he said. "I guess you're right."

Amyla offered her hand and Jayson took it. "Just remember what I said. Don't say the *P* word and you'll be fine. Oh, and don't talk about the money too much either. And don't ask about returning your companion lifeforms."

"And don't feed them after midnight or get them wet. I've got it." He laughed at his own joke, but Amyla didn't seem to get the reference.

"Right."

"It's from—"

"Please proceed to adoption room seven," her indicator repeated.

"I've got to go. Nice meeting you, Jayson."

Amyla grabbed her husband by the arm as she passed by and nearly drug him to the indicated adoption room where her counselor and future awaited.

As they left, Jayson looked up at the giant digital display in the front of the room. It read 1,274,190 successful placements. The number had ticked up a few more since he had arrived. He wondered if there was a separate sign indicating unsuccessful placements.

Jayson looked again at the forms he had completed. Space for companion lifeform: minimal. Time available for training: minimal. Previous experience in xeno-biology: none. Looking at the answers he provided, he wasn't sure he should be allowed to adopt a goldfish, let alone a pair of alien mystery creatures.

"Please proceed to adoption room two." The same holographic model leapt from his indicator. Originally he thought it was a projection of the actual adoption counselor, but since both of his neighbors had the same female image as his own, it must be a generic program.

Jayson hit the acknowledge button on his indicator and grabbed the tablet with his documents. His heart threatened to beat its way right out of his chest. *Not unlike the xenomorph face-hugger he was probably about to adopt*, he thought. He took a few deep breaths to calm his nerves and entered the door marked Adoption Room Two.

The room was small, the center dominated by a large desk with chairs around it. A large video display was mounted on the wall and currently cycled through a slideshow of happy families enjoying time with their new companion lifeforms. It looked about as real as the people in the side-by-side bathtubs discussing their erectile dysfunction in those television commercials.

The adoption specialist rose to his feet when he entered and offered his hand. He was young, barely out of college if Jayson had to guess, and gave off a distinct used car salesman vibe.

"Mr. Lindt? I'm Specialist Alex McDonald. Do please have a seat."

He clicked a few times on the computer and spoke without looking up.

"I see you have a family. Did they join you today for the assignment consultation?"

"No," Jayson said. "They tend to get a bit emotional. I thought it best if I came in alone."

The man looked at Jayson. "So you do not plan to have an emotional attachment to your companion life forms?"

"It isn't that," Jayson added quickly. "I'm sure I will...uh, love the...creatures...as much as the rest of the family. But I think a bit of rational decision making is a good thing. At the beginning."

The young man smiled, fluorescent light bouncing off perfect white teeth. "I couldn't agree more. Far too many people rush into the decision."

He clicked again on the computer and the slideshow disappeared from the monitor to be replaced by the data Jayson had provided earlier about their home and family situation.

"Now, I have had a chance to review your application. Everything seems to be in order, but I do have a few questions."

"Sure."

"First, I want to assure you that although my questions might sound...strange, they are simply to allow us to determine the best placement for you and your family."

"I understand."

"You have read all of the provided literature?"

"Pretty much. Yeah."

The perfect smile flickered for a moment before returning. "Then you are aware that although NASA and the Center for Xenomorphic Studies have thoroughly examined all of the life forms that arrived on Stellar Ark One, the sheer number and variety of species makes it impossible for us to know everything about them. That is why we rely on host families for assistance."

"Right," Jayson said. "We have to study them. And report back?"

"Not study, Mr. Lindt. Just observe as you go about your lives together. You will submit monthly reports back to the Center. Are you agreeable to this?"

"Sure."

"Very well. I will just need your fingerprint as acknowledgement here." McDonald pushed a small scanner forward. Jayson pressed down his thumb and saw the image of his print flash briefly on the screen followed by the word *Acceptance*.

"You must also understand that while the Center will provide what data it has on your chosen companion lifeforms, there will remain unknowns. These unknowns could include diet, life expectancy, behavior, breeding techniques, maximum size, intelligence, and potential psychic potential."

"I'm sorry, did you say—"

"If I could just get your fingerprint again, Mr. Lindt."

Jayson pressed down his thumb. *Acceptance.*

"Finally," McDonald continued mechanically. "The Center agrees to provide a monthly stipend in order to offset any costs incurred by your companion lifeforms. In return, you agree to care for the creatures to the best of your ability, accept responsibility should it be determined you are at fault for any adverse effects the creatures encounter, and relinquish the Center from any liability should your companion lifeforms maim, mutilate, digest, terrorize, dominate, melt, incinerate, disintegrate, or kill, you, your family, acquaintances, or general passersby."

"And does that happen a lot?" Jayson asked. "Things like disintegration, I mean?"

McDonald smiled broadly. "Not a lot. No. Please just press your thumb here."

Acceptance.

"Great!" McDonald typed on the computer and the paperwork disappeared from the screen. "That handles all of that boring legal talk. Now, let's get onto the good stuff, shall we?"

Jayson was feeling a bit numb and having trouble shaking the image of his children melting while playing with their new companion lifeforms.

"Based on the information you provided us, I've selected three options for you to select from. I think any will be great additions to your family."

Jayson nodded. "Alright. Something easy would be nice. My cousin got these silicon—"

"No mineral-based lifeforms today, I'm afraid. Besides, you don't want one of those."

"I don't?"

McDonald shook his head, but kept his smile stapled in place. "Oh no. Terribly boring. Plus, they can die on you and it'll take years to notice. No, I've got much better options for you."

Boring didn't sound so bad, but it was pointless to argue. All Jayson could do was go for the least objectionable of his options. If he heard one word of complaint from Dian or the kids, he was going to lose it.

"Now, I'm particularly excited about this first option." McDonald clicked something on the computer and the display went completely white. He looked to Jayson and smiled. "Amazing, aren't they?"

Jayson squinted and looked harder at the screen. He couldn't see anything apart from a bit of dust on the monitor.

"I'm sorry," Jayson said. "What am I looking at?"

McDonald sighed dramatically and walked up to the display, pointing at the dust Jayson had noticed. "This cloud of particles here. And this here." He pointed at another dusty section of monitor.

Jayson shook his head, uncertain what it was he was supposed to be marveling over.

"Granted, it takes a little getting used to. They're methane-based lifeforms. Let me switch to the video, that'll be easier for you."

He walked over to his computer and hit a few keys. The dust Jayson had previously thought was on the outside of the display started to shift. It blew around, quickly assuming a small vortex shape. The other cloud of dust did likewise until the two tiny tornadoes spun around in tandem, like a pair of Sufi mystics.

"You want me to adopt a pair of...whirlwinds?"

"We at the Center call them Terror Twisters." Jayson didn't know what face he made, but it obviously concerned McDonald. He added quickly, "Terror is perhaps a bit strong. There is no indication they're violent. Or sentient. It's just that they smell like a swamp and have the tendency to suck up small creatures."

"But I have children, Mr. McDonald," Jayson said.

The adoption specialist laughed. "Oh, Mr. Lindt. They could never consume a child. I just meant things like cats, small dogs, guinea pigs, squirrels. Your family would be quite safe, I assure you. I mean, I can't *legally* assure you. It is just a figure of speech."

"Yes, well. They are interesting, but you did say you have two other options?"

McDonald looked disappointed. He watched the video of the tornadoes whip about the screen for a few more seconds before returning to his computer.

"Yes. Let's look at the other options. Perhaps they will be more in your line of thinking."

When the next image came on to the screen, Jayson not only knocked his own chair to the ground as he stumbled back violently in an attempt to escape, but he also sent a large stack of stationery and writing tools flying in his wild flailing.

"Granted, they aren't the most physically attractive lifeforms," McDonald said calmly as though Jayson wasn't lying on the ground, a pile of paper clips and ballpoint pens rolling off him as he attempted to right himself. "They are actually quite sweet. Once you earn their trust, of course."

Jayson pulled his chair back to its feet and sat down. Even now, knowing what he would see on the screen, it was hard to look without urinating.

Something that could euphemistically be described as "slug-like" filled the screen. The skin was mustard yellow and four eyestalks sprung from its head, each ending in a globular eye of a different color. A large vertical slit ran up the center of the body, its edge lined in jagged white teeth, serrated like a shark.

"Is that a mouth?" Jayson asked quietly, pointing toward the orifice.

"Among other things," McDonald answered calmly.

Jayson decided he didn't want all of the specifics. "And how large is this...lifeform anyway?"

McDonald glanced at his notes. "From the tip of its tail to the end of its primary eyestalk, it is three meters."

"I'm sorry," Jayson said. "Did you say meters? This thing is ten feet tall?"

"Nine feet, ten inches, to be exact."

Jayson tried to picture the slug monster slithering around his house, its eyes smacking into every doorway. It would almost serve Dian right if he brought it home. She and the kids wanted a companion so bad? Great. Pass the salt.

"I thought we could only adopt a pair of lifeforms. Is there just one of these...things?"

"You must adopt a breeding group, technically," McDonald clarified. "Generally that is a pair, much like humans. A few of the xenomorphs are asexual and come as individuals. Some actually come in higher multiples. Just yesterday I adopted out a flock of Pygmy Marrow-sucking Eaglerats. They come as a group of seven, all necessary for breeding. Quite fascinating really."

"So this thing is asexual?"

"Oh no. The Lumbering Ooze does come as a pair. The male stalker is smaller, and lives inside the ventral orifice."

Jayson felt queasy. "There is another slug inside that mouth thing?"

McDonald nodded. "I told you it had multiple functions. Are you okay, Mr. Lindt? You look a bit peaky."

"No," Jayson said, swallowing the bile that kept trying to force its way up. "I'm great. You said there was a third option?"

McDonald appeared crestfallen. Jayson felt like he was crushing every one of the man's dreams. He wondered if McDonald would be happy to have a Lumbering Ooze in his backyard.

"There is one more. I selected it really as a back up though." His voice dropped to a whisper. "I'm not supposed to say this, but these guys are really rather boring. A safety, if you will. I understand the Ooze is a bit intimidating, but are you sure you aren't interested in the Terror Twisters?"

"I'm sure," Jayson said. "What is the third option?"

McDonald walked slowly to his computer, his shoulders hanging low. He clicked a button and the display changed to the third possible companion lifeform.

Jayson knew it was a winner.

It was three days before the Center for Xenomorphic Studies could finalize all of the preparations and deliver the new companion lifeforms to the Lindt household. Jayson's family was excited, but furious and frustrated at his unwillingness to tell them anything about their new family members. The kids had begged. Dian had first pleaded, then screamed, then resorted to silence. Through it all, Jayson held firm. They would learn soon enough. They wanted this. They could wait for the results.

The workers from the Center carefully offloaded the crate from the back of the truck. The container was marked with warning labels indicating the contents were "Live Xenomorphs". After signing for delivery, the truck left and the family stood around the crate in the garage. No sound came from inside.

Jayson took the key provided by the delivery team and opened the lock. His family standing around, full of nervous energy. The children looked ready to burst, and his wife gave Jayson a smug smile.

Jayson smiled back at her causing Dian to look uncertain.

When the door opened two creatures stepped out. From all outward appearances, it was a pair of Golden Retrievers. The were the epitome of the breed. Beautiful golden-red coats, perfectly proportioned, with one of the two slightly larger than the other. If this was Westminster, these dogs would tie for Best in Show.

"I don't understand," Dian said. The kids looked similarly baffled. "You got us dogs?"

"No," Jayson said. "They aren't dogs. They are Garrulous Space Hounds."

"Garru..." his daughter tried to repeat.

"They're *dogs*, dad," his son said. "You promised us xenomorphs. You promised!"

"I told you, they're not dogs."

"I *knew* you would screw this up, Jayson. I just knew it. I never should have let you go alone. Did you even go? Did you chicken out at the last moment and think you could fool us with this?" She waved her hands toward the two dogs, who both sat panting. "This nonsense? Well, you can take them back."

"I can't take them back, Dian," Jayson said. "It's in the adoption contract. You know that. They're ours for life."

"Stop, Jayson. Just stop. These are not the pets we wanted. We all agreed that—"

"*Companion life form*," said the larger of the two space hounds.

"Yes," said the other. "There is no need to be rude."

All of the color drained from Dian's face.

"Did that dog just say something?" she asked quietly.

"Garrulous Space Hound," Jayson repeated. "Garrulous. As in talkative."

"But dogs can't..." Dian trailed off. I thought she might faint.

"Talk?" said the larger space hound, his voice deep. He seemed to be the male. "That's true, but we're not dogs."

"You weren't kidding," the smaller space hound said, looking up to Jayson. "She is a bit slow."

"Now, I didn't say that." Jayson laughed. "Not exactly."

Dian still looked from her husband to the space hounds to the children. "These are xenomorphs?"

Jayson sighed. She and the kids had wanted this. "You would have preferred a Lumbering Ooze?"

The smaller space hound shivered. "Trust me. You do *not* want one of those in your house."

"So," the larger hound said. "Are we going in or what? I don't do garages. I'm going to need a sofa, the bigger the better. And I'm hungry. I only eat organic, by the way."

"I think we're going to like it here, Frank," the smaller space hound said to her partner. "These people seem nice. Or will, with some training."

The larger space hound stood and walked over to Jayson's daughter. He gave her a giant lick across the cheek, his tongue pink and wet.

"Yeah," the space hound said. "I think this will do nicely. Come on, Betty. Let's check out the house."

Shawn Kobb is an American diplomat who has lived, worked, and traveled the world. He uses this experience to fuel his writing. You can find out more about his writing at shawnkobb.com. He is currently living in Budapest, Hungary.

Wyldblood Magazine #5 available for pre-order!

If you like what you're reading and want to see more you can sign up to the next issue for delivery direct to your door or inbox.

£5.99/$7.99 print or £2.99/$3.99 digital.

www.wyldblood.com/magazine

Seventy Miles from Phoenix
David Dixon

Michael squints as he stares west down I-10, snapped like a black chalk line across the parched brown desert. The rising heat blurs the horizon into shimmering waves, and I-10 vanishes skyward, blending into undulating black lines, an infinite series of distant, writhing snakes.

"See it?" Caesar says.

"No."

"It's coming."

Caesar would see it. After all, he has the binoculars.

"You sure?"

"*Si.*"

Caesar doesn't say anything else. That isn't unusual; the heat sucks the life out of everything—plants, people, animals, conversation. Michael used to speak in more than monosyllables, he thinks, but he can't say for sure. Even though he's only been in the RT for a few months, sometimes it's hard to remember what life was like back in Chicago, back when he'd been soft, back when living was easy.

He keeps his eyes on the horizon, squinting even though he's wearing polarized sunglasses. He glances at Caesar, his binoculars now dangling around his neck. Caesar never squints, even without sunglasses. Early on, Michael had asked him how he did that, how he stared into the brightness of the desert without flinching. *"Porque no soy una pequeña perra"* had been his answer.

Michael didn't ask Caesar too many questions after that.

After another minute of silence, Michael finally sees it: a dark speck on the horizon, rippling in the heat and growing larger.

A truck.

"I see it," he says.

"Good."

Caesar passes him the binoculars, and Michael trains them on the truck.

It's a big one, hauling four trailers one after the other, barrelling down I-10 at ninety miles an hour. The tractor itself is sleek and black and bullet-shaped, and Michael can just make out the Alibaba logo on its aerodynamic shell.

"What kind is it?" Caesar asks.

Michael adjusts the binoculars and strains to find a manufacturer's logo. "I dunno, can't tell." He finds a red oval with writing low on the shell, but he can't hold the binoculars steady enough to read it. "There's a red circle—oval, really—and there's writing, but I can't tell what—"

"Peterbilt," Caesar says. "Is there a sensor pod up high? Left or right side?"

Michael scans upwards. "Left side."

"Whip antennas or dish?" Caesar asks. "Toward the back. Might even be on the first trailer."

"Ahhh… looks like whip antennas. Two of 'em, other side of the sensor pod."

Caesar grunts.

Michael has spent enough weeks around Caesar to know that isn't good. He looks away from the binoculars. "What?"

"Can't ride it," Caesar says. He casts a worried glance up at the sun, high and merciless overhead. "We gotta go back soon. Half an hour more, maybe."

Michael takes another look at the truck with his binoculars, now close enough for him to read the registration stickers down the side. Unlike some of the rigs he's seen before, it doesn't have anti-climb spikes, or roof ridges that make it impossible to rest on top. "Why not? What's wrong with it? No anti-ride gear on it. I thought you said this morning that—"

"It's a Trump Truck, *ese*. It don't *need* gear. The other trucks? Yeah, sure. But a Trump Truck don't need it 'cuz you can't stop it. You try to get in its way and—" Caesar smashes a tattooed fist into his brown, calloused palm.

"I thought you said they had to stop. This morning, before we left camp, you said we could stop one easy," Michael protests. He's sweating—well, he's been sweating because that's all anybody does in the RT, but now he's *really* sweating. It's a three-hour walk back to camp, and they made the trek out here mostly under the cover of darkness. The thought of walking back in daylight doesn't sit well at all.

"Most of 'em, they do gotta stop. But not the Trump Trucks. When that fine-ass bitch was President, she had 'em change the rules, but only for those four years, you know? So you gotta be careful, gotta pay attention, *ese*. Anything from '32 to '36, you gonna get crushed. Last mistake anybody ever makes in the RT, trying to ride a Trump Truck."

"Shit," Michael mutters.

"Yeah."

The truck is bearing down on them now, the musical hum of its tires growing louder as it nears. It gives a cursory blast of its horn when it comes within a half a mile of them, but doesn't slow. Michael snaps his head to look as it zips past, bringing a welcome blast of wind in its wake. The breeze isn't cool, given that the temperature hovers near 140 degrees, but at least it breaks up the oppressive stillness of the desert.

Caesar stares after it a moment before he picks up his dusty olive-drab rucksack and cinches it to his back. Next comes his anti-drone rifle, used to keep prying eyes away from Caesar's extralegal activities. The rifle consists of a pair of four-foot-long, flat antennas about three inches wide connected by homemade wiring to a bulky battery in the stock, the whole thing held together by duct tape and hatred, judging by the curses in Spanish and English stenciled down the side of the antennas. Caesar slings it over his shoulder and nods south, back the way they came. "Come on. No point waiting any longer. I thought we'd already be gone. Must be a slow day for rich people ordering shit."

"I thought you said we had half an hour more," Michael says. Caesar shrugs.

Michael sighs, dreading the grueling walk back to camp. Before he reaches for his own backpack, though, he takes one more look west through the binoculars. A smile cracks his sun-chapped lips.

"There's another truck."

Caesar extends a hand, and Michael gives him the heavy, rubber-coated binoculars so he can scope out their prey.

"Get ready, *mijo*."

That's a good sign. Caesar only calls anybody *mijo* when he's in a good mood.

Michael unzips his pack and takes out the metallic space blanket Caesar gave him to carry, along with a can of yellow spray paint. He unfolds the blanket across the middle of the eastbound lanes, wincing as it reflects the sunlight like a mirror. "All right, I got—"

"Remember what I said?" Caesar asks. "Put the circles *before* the lines, 'cuz if you fuck it up and—"

"I remember," Michael interrupts. They'd only been over it a hundred times.

"Okay. Then what the hell you doin' standing here?" Caesar asks.

Michael shakes his head and mutters a curse, then grabs the paint and starts to jog west toward the approaching truck.

"Yo," Caesar calls. "Don't forget your water. It's farther than you think. I ain't dragging your ass back."

Michael pulls a plastic two-quart canteen from a side pouch in his backpack, takes a swallow of water so hot it's sweet, then slings it over his side with a strap and takes off down the interstate.

By the time he's made it an eighth of a mile, Michael is glad Caesar told him to bring the canteen. He's sweating so hard now that it's pouring down his face, stinging his eyes, and the brief jog in the heat is enough to make him gasp for breath. He takes another swig before he keeps on jogging until he reaches what he reckons to be the quarter mile Caesar has insisted on. There, he uses the spray paint to decorate the road with a pair of two-foot yellow circles four feet apart, followed by a pair of heavy yellow lines.

By now, the truck is close enough for Michael to see that it's an Amazon Prime truck in blue and white livery, but he can't make out what the make and model are. Still, if Caesar says it'll stop, he knows it will.

Michael sprints back to the space blanket as the truck draws closer. The stifling heat is ever present, and running makes it that much worse. He feels his meager breakfast rising in his throat.

"Careful now, *mijo*," Caesar calls with a smile from where he stands in the middle of the space blanket.

For a moment, Michael hesitates. Caesar watches him, his dark brown eyes revealing nothing, but Michael knows what he's thinking.

This is a test of sorts. Caesar doesn't need Michael to stop the truck. Hell, Caesar has done it by himself a hundred times, probably. But Michael knows it's not about that. Caesar has been good to him since he's come to the RT, and here the RT, you live and die by three things—your friends, your word, and your guts. But the first two aren't worth a damn without the last one, and that's what Caesar is looking to find.

Michael steps into the eastbound lanes and stands next to Caesar, staring into the face of the oncoming truck as it speeds toward them. Michael's heart pounds, even though he knows it shouldn't, even though he knows he can trust Caesar to get it right.

When the truck reaches Michael's painted marks, the truck's brakes whine as it recoups some of the braking energy for the motor's batteries. Michael grins, and his heart rate slows a bit.

The truck's sensors pick them up, and it honks three times in protest as it comes to a complete stop fifteen feet in front of them. The truck's electric motor is silent, save for a fan whirring somewhere deep inside the tractor, cocooned completely in its aerodynamic cowl.

"See? Works every time," Caesar says, nodding at the space blanket. He'd explained it to Michael back at camp last week. Even though the trucks were programmed to stop for any pedestrians in the road, sometimes their cameras had a little difficulty picking people out against the asphalt—Caesar seemed to think the companies did it on purpose—but the metallic space blanket highlighted the contrast and made sure the autopilot recognized them as people. The paint symbols he'd sent Michael to lay down warned the truck of potential pedestrians ahead, which sent it into its more cautious, big-city safe mode instead of its normal high-speed long-haul mode.

"Never doubted you," Michael says.

Caesar barks a laugh. "You were ready to shit your pants. *No la mientas a un mentiroso.* Now, fold up the blanket but don't move just yet."

Michael does as instructed while Caesar tosses a rope ladder with heavy earth magnets on one end up to the roof of the first trailer.

"Caution," the truck warns loudly in a disembodied female voice. "Attempting to ride, hijack, damage, or otherwise interfere with the operation of this automated truck is a crime, and will subject you to criminal penalties which vary by jurisdiction. Additionally, you will be subject to civil penalties by Amazon Incorporated, and your Prime membership will be canceled if you are a member."

"I know, baby," Caesar says to the truck, patting the tractor's fiberglass shell. "But I ain't a member, so I could give a fuck." He tugs on the rope ladder, which doesn't move, then walks back to Michael. "Grab your shit, *ese.* Time to ride."

Michael stuffs the blanket back into his pack, then throws it over his shoulders. He takes Caesar's place in front of the truck while Caesar straps on his rucksack and hoists his drone-rifle. Caesar climbs the ladder to the trailer roof and looks down over the front of the tractor.

"All right, we're good. When you get about five feet behind the sensor pod—" he jerks his head towards a sleek bulbous shape high on the left side of the tractor "—she'll start to move, so don't be surprised. Climb on up. They take a little time to get going."

Michael nods and trots to the ladder. Just as Caesar predicted, the truck starts to roll almost as soon as he's no longer in front of it, but Michael has no problem climbing the thirty feet to the top of the trailer. Once he gets there, he's pleased to find a pair of makeshift reclining chairs bolted to the trailer roof, allowing him to lie down comfortably and still be tucked below the top of the tractor's cowl so there's no danger of being blown off when the truck is at full speed.

"She's a slut." Caesar pats the trailer beneath them as the truck picks up speed. "Been ridden a lot. Nice to have these seats on your first trip, but don't get used to it."

"I'm surprised they don't take 'em off." Michael slides into one, rolling halfway over so he can shrug off his backpack, which he secures to a hook someone has attached to the seat for just that purpose.

"They do," Caesar answers. "When they find 'em. But these things drive and park themselves, and the maintenance and loading and shit is all robot, too, so it's not like they're really getting a lot of eyes on it, you know?" Caesar takes a swig of his canteen, tucks his hands behind his head, and closes his eyes. He's asleep in seconds.

Michael tries to do the same, and between the air rushing around him to keep him cool and the shade of the cowl over his head, he expects to find it easy to sleep, but, unlike Caesar, he's not used to the motion or the noise, so he stays awake.

He keeps his eyes closed and thinks of Chicago and his mom's warning when he told her he was heading to the Restricted Territory. He can't help but smile. Sure, there were some rough times early on, but he's been with Caesar and his crew for a month, and he'd make more in a year with him than he'd make in a decade working some dead-end shift job up in Chicago competing with robots for his bread—if he'd managed to get a job at all.

Something interrupts the sun's light for a moment, and Michael's blood runs cold. His eyes snap open. Birds were rare this far south these days, which can only mean one thing.

Drones.

"Caesar, man, wake up," Michael shouts over the roar of the wind, sitting up and using his hand to shield his eyes as he scans the cloudless blue sky. I think we got some eyes on us."

Caesar is awake in a flash, and already reaching for his drone-rifle. "Fuck."

"Yeah."

They scan the sky for several minutes, but the drone doesn't reappear.

"You sure you saw one?" Caesar asks.

"I mean… no, not exactly," Michael says, feeling stupid. "But there was a shadow, and I figure that—"

"Yeah, it does," Caesar says. "But it might not be watching the road. There's other types, too."

Michael nods, looking back over the next four trailers strung out behind the one they're on, and looking farther back down the arrow-straight strip of I-10 behind them. "How long to Phoenix?" he asks, leaning close so Caesar can hear him. He'll feel better when they reach the city. Officially, it's abandoned, like the rest of the RT, but at least there the surveillance drones find it harder to track people among the skeletons of the skyscrapers.

Caesar doesn't answer. Instead, he pokes his head around the left side of the truck, exposing his face to the full force of the wind before retreating back under the fiberglass shield. "Not much longer," he says, leaning close to Michael. "Highway 60 is coming up in a mile or two, off to the left. From there it's like a hundred miles to Phoenix, tops. So, like, maybe an hour or so."

Caesar lies back down and is asleep in no time again, but Michael drinks some water and eats a long-expired energy bar to quiet his growling stomach. He's lost a lot of weight since he came to the RT, but he still can't match Caesar's seemingly unflagging energy no matter the heat or lack of food and

water. He stares off to the west, wondering if they'll ever have reason to go all the way to the coast. He'd like that, he thinks. He's never seen the ocean except on TV, and even though the Great Lakes are *like* the ocean, they *aren't* the ocean.

Something catches his eye behind them, and he cocks his head to the side to stare at it. There's another vehicle on the road, but it doesn't look big enough to be a truck and—

His heart almost stops.

Flashing lights.

"Caesar, Caesar," he shouts. "The cops!"

Again, Caesar startles awake, and this time there's no denying it. They've been made, somehow. "*Ay chingados,*" he mutters. "Okay, *ese,* listen up. Here's how it's gonna be. When he gets close, he's gonna send his magic 5-0 signal and the truck is gonna stop. When it slows down to like twenty miles an hour, we jump. He won't look for us if we head off into the desert because he really doesn't care. He just wants us off the truck. But if he catches us while we're still aboard? That shit ain't good, *ese.*"

"*Jump?*" Michael asks incredulously. "I'll break my fucking neck!"

Caesar shakes his head. "It's the only way. I've done it before. You just gotta tuck and roll when you hit."

"Fuck fuck fuck," Michael says. "*Fuck.*"

The flashing red and blue lights get closer and closer, and Michael feels his stomach tightening. This can't be happening. Who the fuck cares if they ride a goddamn truck to Phoenix? Nobody is supposed to be out here in the first fucking place. Where the *fuck* did the cop come from?

From somewhere underneath them, there's an audible electronic *ding,* and the truck starts to slow. The angular black cop car is even closer now, so close Michael can make out its tinted windshield and gleaming chrome detail work. A shadow passes overhead, and Michael looks up out of instinct. A black octocopter zips overhead and matches speed with the police car before lowering itself back into its docking cradle on the back side of the cruiser.

"You ready?" Caesar asks. He's edging toward the side of the trailer, ready to toss his backpack over the side.

Michael nods, even though he doesn't mean it. His tongue is a sandpaper block in his mouth, and when he looks over the side of the truck at the desert rushing by, all he can picture is himself as a bloodied heap by the side of the road.

The truck is moving so slowly by now that the heat has returned, and with a vengeance. After the half hour or so they spent in the wind, the scorching sun is even worse than before.

"It's time to go, *ese*." Caesar tosses his rucksack off first, then half a second later his rifle.

"I don't know if I can—"

Michael doesn't get time to finish his sentence. Caesar jumps.

Michael scrambles over to the left side of the truck, but he can't see Caesar. His dusty white dishdasha has already blended into the dirt, and the truck continues to move. Michael grabs his backpack and readies himself, resisting the urge to throw up.

The truck shifts under his feet, and he collapses backward onto the trailer rather than allowing himself to pitch over the side. The truck slows further as it pulls off into the right shoulder. Michael contemplates jumping again before the squelch of a siren freezes him in his tracks.

The cop car has arrived, a late-model Ford in all black, save a silver *RTCSS*—Restricted Territory Contracted Security Services— down the side. The red and blue lights reflect off the white of the trailer, and Michael's life flashes before his eyes. He doesn't know what the penalty for truck-hopping is, but he knows it's probably a few months' jail time at the least, and once he goes in, he knows he'll have to start all over again when he gets out.

He should have jumped, like Caesar said. Goddamn it, where was his courage from earlier?

He stands up, preparing to make a run and leap off the right side of the trailer.

"Don't even think about it," the cop says over his car's loudspeaker. As if to emphasize the futility of such an attempt, the menacing octocopter lifts off with a buzz and hovers over the trailer. "Stay right where you are and put your hands over your head."

Michael does so, a million excuses running through his head. He'd gotten out of trouble with cops in Chicago before, but somehow, he knows that down here in the RT things are different.

The driver's side gullwing door slides up, and the cop steps out—a tall, well-built white guy in his mid-thirties with close cropped hair, black ballistic-lensed sunglasses, and a no-nonsense frown on his face. Unlike Michael and Caesar who are dressed in loose-fitting man dresses and brown boots—pretty much standard uniform for the RT—the cop is in more traditional attire. Gray fatigues under a black tactical vest, with a pistol on his right hip and a taser on his left.

The cop walks to the edge of the trailer, not taking his gaze off Michael.

Michael's knees are trembling and he can hear his heartbeat in his ears. Darkness creeps into his vision, closing on him like a tunnel, but he isn't sure if it's heat exhaustion or dehydration or fear. *Just let me go.*

For a moment, the cop says nothing. Then, with a slight flick of his eyes toward his cruiser, he says, "Dispatch, this is Two-Niner Alpha."

"This is dispatch," a male voice answers from his car speaker. "Go 'head."

"Roger. Cut my cameras and voice feed, would you? I'm going ten-seven for a bit."

The dispatcher chuckles. "Again? Fourth time today. Whatcha been up to that's gotcha so busy you need to take breaks?"

"You know how it is, dispatch. Just gotta take care of something real quick."

There's an electronic chime from somewhere in the car. "Ten-four, Two-Niner Alpha. I cut your feed and video. I always do my best work when I'm on break, you know?"

"Me too," the cop replies. His wicked grin makes Michael's breath catch in his throat.

"Dispatch out," the dispatcher says.

The cop stares at Michael. "Jump on down here, toasty," the cop says. Part of Michael is proud, for a fleeting moment, that he's been mistaken as a local.

"O-okay." Michael turns toward the rope ladder behind him.

"*Stop*," the cop says, hand on his pistol. "Where the fuck are you going?"

"I'm coming down, like you said."

"Not that way, chucklefuck," the cop says. "*This* way. I said *jump*, just like your dumbass toasty friend did back there. Speaking of which—Two-Niner UAV, go find our second suspect. Authorization one-four-eight-eight."

"Acknowledged," a computer voice says from the octocopter overhead, and it zips west down I-10 with a muted whir of rotors.

The cop stares up at Michael. "Well? Are you gonna jump down like I said, or am I gonna have to shoot your dumb ass to get you down?"

"W-what?" Michael asks, his hands still above his head. "I don't—"

"*Ten… nine…*" the cop intones, drawing his pistol.

"It's a long way down!"

"*Eight… three…*" The cop raises his pistol.

Michael's feet move before his brain has time to give any conscious instructions, and he finds himself plummeting toward the pavement.

He lands like a sack of wet shit.

A bolt of pain stabs through his right ankle, and even without looking at it, he knows it's broken. "Fuuuuuck," he whimpers through clenched teeth. Wincing, he reaches for his ankle, but a kick to his ribcage knocks the breath out of him. He rolls over on his back and looks up at the cop, who's silhouetted against the noonday sun in the shade of the trailer.

"The fuck are you doing?" the cop asks.

"My… my ankle. I think it's broken," Michael whispers.

"I don't give a fuck. I didn't tell you to move, did I?"

"N-no."

"Then don't fucking move. Jesus, you toasties are fucking dumber than a bag of hammers. *Don't. Move.*" He looks over his shoulder back at his cruiser. "Computer, release the stopped truck. Authorization one-four-eight-eight."

"Acknowledged," the computer voice says again.

The Amazon transfer truck starts rolling again with a crunch of tires against the dirt. The shade disappears when the last trailer pulls past him, leaving Michael sprawled out on the hot asphalt, baking in the sun.

Waves of nausea wash over him, but he doesn't make a move to tend to his ankle or shield his eyes. He doesn't need another kick from the cop.

The officer stands over him and bends down to retrieve his backpack. He sifts through it, then tosses it on the hood of his car. "You got any drugs on you?"

Michael shakes his head. It's actually true. This time.

The cop frowns at him. "Don't you know it's illegal to truck-hop? They're not your trucks. Hell, you're not even supposed to be out in the RT without a permit anyway. You got a permit?"

Another shake of Michael's head.

"Of course you don't, you stupid-ass toasty. So what should I do? Arrest you? You wanna get arrested?"

Michael shakes his head a third time.

The cop smiles. "Well, good. 'Cause I'm not going to. It'd be a waste of my time and your time. You'd just go back, get booked, then released, and be back out here with your stupid-ass toasty friends the next day for me to catch again tomorrow. Plus, you'd never show up to court anyway, so what's the point, right? Right?"

The cop steps on his broken ankle.

Michael screams as a supernova of agony explodes through his body. It hurts like nothing else he's ever felt before. Nothing but searing pain. That's all the world is—hurt. There's no road, no sun, no desert, no backpack, no Caesar. There is only the cop's boot, pressing hard on his already-broken ankle. Michael's vision flashes white, and he vomits up his energy bar until he dry heaves.

"Goddamn are you making a mess," the cop says as he mercifully steps off Michael's ankle. "A total fucking mess."

Michael is only dimly aware of the officer's presence as he leans over him and jerks on his canteen. The cop pulls so hard he lifts Michael's body partway off the pavement, then drops him again, shooting stars across his vision when his head hits the asphalt.

"Give it to me," the cop says.

Michael fumbles with the strap and manages to gingerly tug the canteen up his chest and over his head. He extends it with a weak arm toward the cop.

The officer takes it and unscrews the lid. "I'm gonna let you go. I will. But not until after we clean up this mess you've made." He dumps the canteen onto the asphalt, and Michael suddenly understands.

It ends here.

The cop chuckles. "I see you're finally getting it." He tosses the empty canteen back into Michael's chest. "You're free to go. I'm not gonna arrest you." He looks overhead. "Of course, it is mighty hot—computer, what's the temperature?"

"One-hundred and forty-one degrees Fahrenheit," it answers.

The officer kneels down to look at Michael. "You might want to get walking, son. I reckon you got another seventy miles or so to Phoenix, at least. I don't know where you came from, but I figure it can't be close either. Best of luck to you, toasty."

He stands with a chuckle.

"Wait," Michael rasps.

"Nope."

Michael doesn't want to—doesn't want to give the asshole the satisfaction—but he can't stop himself. His tears, his precious water, drip down to the asphalt. He drags himself to a sitting position as the cop watches, leaning against the hood of his cruiser with his arms folded.

"Go ahead. Get going," the officer says.

Michael wipes his tears on his dishdasha sleeve and grits his teeth. He tries to stand, but his ankle won't take the weight. Even the slightest pressure makes his vision grow dark. He gives it another shot before the pain collapses him back to the pavement.

He stares at the cop for a moment, then spits.

The cop laughs. "Come an hour or so from now in his heat, you'll be wishing you could lick that off the interstate, you dumb fuck."

A flash of movement catches Michael's eye, and there's a second of confusion before he realizes what's happening.

The cop never sees it coming.

The butt of Caesar's anti-drone rifle smashes against the officers's head, driving him forward to the asphalt. He tries to roll over, but Caesar is too fast. The buttstock crashes into the back of the cop's head, and Micheal watches in terrified awe as Caesar snatches the cop's pistol out of his belt.

"You all right down there?" Caesar asks Michael, anti-drone rifle in his left hand, pistol in his right. "Next time I say jump, you gonna listen, huh, *ese*?"

"Y-yeah," Michael replies, wincing in pain.

Caesar laughs. "Good, 'cause I ain't gonna pull your dumb ass out the fire again."

The cop groans and tries to roll over again, before Caesar pistol whips him. "Shut up, *la hija de puta estúpida*. I got the gun now. That'll teach you to send a drone to do a man's job. Come after Caesar with a fuckin' octocopter?" He kicks the cop.

The officer says something, but Michael is too far away and in too much pain to make it out.

"I know," Caesar replies. "I ain't trying to. I'm just gonna borrow it for a minute. You can pick it up in Phoenix." His sadistic smile gleams. "Of course, you gonna have to walk there to get it, just like you told my man Michael here. See you in hell, fucker."

Paul comes to fifteen minutes later.

His head throbs and it hurts to even think, but what worries him most is the feeling of sunburn on his exposed arms and neck. All the water he has is in his car, which those two goddamn toasties had now, cruising toward Phoenix. If he doesn't get moving and find shade quick, he's not going to make it to nightfall.

He tries to radio for help, but his radio is tied to his car and they've either cut the comms off completely or it's out of range. He calls for the octocopter, because it's got a relay that might reach dispatch, but he gets nothing.

Stupid fucking vindictive toasties.

He staggers to his feet and looks east toward Phoenix, the horizon an unbroken line of shimmering heatwaves, then back west, where the horizon is much the same.

"Fuck."

He shrugs out of his tactical vest and unbuttons his shirt. Belatedly, he realizes one of them even took his sunglasses.

Jesus Christ, when I get back to dispatch I'm going to track those two fuckers till the ends of the earth.

A distortion in the heat to the west sends his heart singing. There's a truck on the road!

Out of habit, he reaches for his eStop Stick, then realizes it too is in his car. He mutters a curse as he stares down the approaching truck, then shrugs.

Fuck it. He's seen it done by toasties a million times, and they even practiced it once or twice at the police academy. *Make yourself unmistakably visible and walk directly toward the vehicle, keeping its sensor pod(s) as much in view as possible,* he remembers the police manual saying. *Raise a sign of distress, which autopilots are required by law to acknowledge.* He strips off his shirt and swings it around his head as he walks down the highway toward the truck. *The vehicle will slow upon recognizing a human in need of assistance, and will stop if the human does not move, as required first by the Gomez-Thompson Act of 2023 and then by the Return to Safe Roads Act of 2039.*

"Hey!" Paul shouts at the approaching truck. "Hey, I need a lift or at least your radio!"

The truck is close now. It doesn't seem to be slowing down much, but then again, these things can practically stop on a dime, and they aren't programmed to stop a moment before they had to.

It honks at him twice, and he smiles.

His face falls as something else from the police manual springs to mind. *Use caution when approaching automated trucks built during the Ivanka Trump Administration (2032–2036), as their programming is not required by law to be Gomez-Thompson or Return to Safe Roads compliant.*

The 2036 Kenworth T1270's autopilot registers a disturbance at 1415L, when it strikes an unauthorized pedestrian in the eastbound lane of I-10, 112.7 kilometers — roughly seventy miles — from Phoenix.

It doesn't slow down.

*David Dixon is a veteran and author living with his family in Springfield, Virginia. His debut novel, *The Damsel* was published by Kyanite Press in November 2020; his short fiction appeared in Middle West Press's *Our Best War Stories,* and in the June edition of Common Tongue Magazine.*

Watch
Film and TV

Loki
Disney+

Army of the Dead
Netflix

I love a good formulaic zombie romp, and this one's got Drax the Destroyer in it, so what's not to like? Not actually Drax, of course, but the guy who plays him in the MCU, Dave Bautista, looking all pumped up and angry as he leads an improbable mission into zombie-infested Las Vegas to bludgeon through an audacious casino heist before the authorities rain down nuclear hell.

There's daughters in danger, there's double crossing good/bad guys, there's sacrifice, there's death defying rescues, there's redemption and there are a whole townsworth of zombies, some deader than others. They're bright, some of these zombies, can speak (ish), have babies and move fast. Oh and there's a very cool zombie tiger for the heroes to get through.

It's directed by Zack Snyder, who I'd worried had seriously lost the plot after his turgid *Justice League* director's cut, but this film is all that Justice League wasn't – fast paced, entertaining and a whole lot of fun. Watch on Netflix – and watch out for the scheduled prequel.

This much anticipated Marvel series has finally arrived on Disney +, with the God of Mischief miraculously resurrected from having his neck snapped by Thanos (all about variant timelines, naturally – which hopefully means we can see some other resurrections too, since death in the comics is rarely permanent). Disney+ have already developed an impressive track record with these small-screen outings, which seem to get better and better. And, unlike both *WandaVision and The Falcon and the Winter Soldier*, *Loki* isn't a one-off: there's a second season scheduled and, hopefully, many more to come.

The plot's convoluted (and very *Dr Who*). Loki gets snatched from the timeline by the Time Variance Authority (TVA - very 'Time Lords') and given a hard choice: be erased as a 'variant' or join forces with them to fix the timeline from a threat that turns out to be other variants of himself. Owen Wilson stars as Mobius, a TVA agent who quickly realises he's been kept in the dark about what's actually happening. Richard E Grant's in it to, as a Loki variant dressed up in a badly fitting traditional Loki costume (from the comic books) and, (very Doctor's companion), Sophia Di Martino plays a female Loki variant (apparently – but I feel a twist coming) who gives Loki the chance to fall in love with himself. Since he's a classic narcissist this is deliciously apposite.

Love the humour in this show. Love the casting, the setting, the twisty-turny plotline, the obvious *Dr Who* touches, the pace, the style, the tone. Love everything about it. More *Loki*, please, on big screen and small. Streaming on Disney+ now.

The Tomorrow War
Amazon Prime

You'd have thought anything with Chris Pratt in it would be good, right? Funny and engaging, though not even slightly serious, Pratt's appeared in some highly entertaining blockbusters like the *Guardians of the Galaxy* and *Jurassic World*. And then there's *The Tomorrow War*. Great if you like extended sequences of aliens being ineffectually shot at with very loud machine gun rounds. Great if you like convoluted time travel plots that don't even nod at the massive temporal paradox plot holes that should swamp the whole storyline. Great if you like your bad guys one-dimensional and your good guys generational screwups who find redemption. Great if you like your alien sound effects recycled from a gazillion other movies. You get the picture.

Plotwise this is a story about aliens suddenly appearing in the future and wiping out most of humanity. Running short of troops for the fightback, the remaining humans reach back into the past and conscript thousands of 2022 people for seven day missions to waste ammunition against the impervious carapaces of the aliens. Dan Forester (Pratt) jumps forward in time to save the day. The leader of the future troops is, inevitably, Dan's estranged daughter. So he's got family conflicts to sort out before he can save the world.

With its fine cast and cool premise this film should have worked, but it easily falls into well- worn tropes and sacrifices credibility for (pointless) action sequences. Which isn't to say it doesn't have its moments, and if you like all action movies this might be for you.

Sweet Tooth
Netflix

Hidden Gem, this one. A comic book adaptation (as huge amounts of the streamer's SF&F seems to be) but not one I was familiar with (it's on DC's Vertigo imprint). It's set in a post-apocalyptic world of pollution, disease and mutations. Most people die and babies (not that there are many of those any more) stop being fully human – something animal's crept in. Most of these 'hybrids' are shunned, ignored, hunted or exploited (if they're lucky). Gus – the 'Sweet Tooth of the title – is a hybrid human/deer is raised in hiding until his father dies. He then searches for his mother, who disappeared many years before and who he believes is in the mysterious land of 'Colorado'. That brings him into contact with the big bad big wide world, full of post-apocalyptic dregs and warlords, including the mean and menacing General Abbott. There's an interesting side plot with a doctor keeping his infected wife alive by using an experimental compound he discovers is from dead hybrids – which leads to all sorts of moral complications. There's Last Men and an Animal Army plus some cute (and some not so cute) hybrids all making this an inventive and dynamic series, all carried along by a strong plotline, plenty of tension, some engaging characters and a strong lead performance from young Christian Convery, who plays Sweet Tooth.

Eight episodes and more to come. 98% on Rottem Tomatoes, so don't just take our word for it. Find it on Netflix.

Read
Books

Shards of Earth
Adrian Tchaikovsky

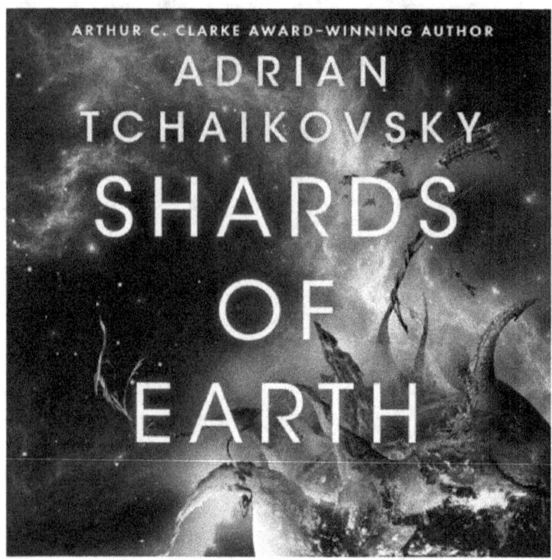

The latest from the prolific Adrian Tchaikovsky, *Shards of Earth* is high-tech, high concept space opera filling out almost 550 fast paced pages with imaginative plotlines, quirky characters and solid science fiction. Set in space, in the future, in a galaxy populated by humans and decidedly non-humanoid aliens, it's the first of a trilogy, so happily there's more to come.

The main character is an Intermediary (or 'Int') called Idris, who's one of a small cadre of specially crafted humans who can safely navigate 'unspace' without going mad. He navigates for itinerant traders on the decrepit cargo ship the *Vulture God* and generally tries to stay out of trouble.

Years before, he was at the centre of a war with aliens called the Architects, whose modus operandi was to send big ships to populated planets and remodel them into massive works of art (albeit killing everyone in the process). Earth is destroyed, and human populated worlds across the galaxy are at risk. Idris managed to infiltrate the mind of an Architect as the giant ship prepared to destroy the new human capital planet, Berlenhof, following which the Architects withdrew. Humanity, thinking they were gone for good, rebuilt. But then a ship emerges from unspace, destroyed and reshaped apparently by the Architects hands and panic resumes.

During the first conflict with the Architects, a band of gene modified female fighters, the Parthenon, sacrifice much to keep humanity safe, but they're shunned in the new order – one of their best, Solace, revisits old acquaintances with Idris and becomes part of the *Vulture God* team and those two characters are pivotal in driving the plot,. Rounding out the crew are an add mix of aliens and misfits. Much of this is well worn territory but it's executed well and it's nice to see a character with disabilities (Olli) given such a prominent and positive role.

And there's a mad alien cult led by an alien gangster determined to wreck everything called, delightfully, the Unspeakable Aklu, the Razor and the Hook. Great stuff.

MB

Q
Christina Dalcher

Described as a 'dystopian thriller', 'Q' is the second novel from Dalcher and follows her successful 2018 debut work 'Vox'.

The premise is this: society is now run by your 'Q' score; the school that children go to is dependent upon what they score in monthly tests. The lowest scorers are forced to go to boarding school hundreds of miles away. Parents are forced to comply; if they don't go along with it, their own scores will be lowered and their jobs and homes could be taken away.

Teachers focus on the gifted and our protagonist Elena Fairchild is one such teacher, working at one of the country's elite schools. Every morning, school buses in the corresponding colours for each school – Silver, Green or Yellow – come to pick up the children. If a child has received a low Q score – they board the `Yellow' bus and are rarely seen again.

All well and good, until we learn that Elena faked the pre-natal test score for her second daughter as she couldn't bear the consequences if the score was not acceptable. And now, her daughter is failing the monthly tests and is about to be shipped off to a Yellow school.

Elena keeps telling herself that this isn't really about eugenics. But when she manages to get demoted in order to be with her daughter at a Yellow school, she discovers that what is going on is far more terrifying that she could have imagined.

The political messages are clear in this fast-paced read. Segregation by intellect, combined with the concept of breeding for an improved world. Dalcher draws on the history of Nazi Germany and the American Eugenics Movement to provide a thought provoking and chilling narrative.

As I mentioned, this is a fast paced read – as a result, some of the characters are not as developed as they could be and we do not get the benefit of another point of view. We also lose the benefit of detail, which makes it difficult at times to buy into this dystopian world. Some of the writing is a little clumsy at times and I wonder if the writer is a little out of her depth with her chosen subject matter.

That said, 'Q' is a compelling, disturbing and intriguing novel. If, like me, you enjoy dystopian fiction stories featuring a strong female lead, it's definitely worth a look.

SDB

The Sunken Land Begins to Rise Again
M. John Harrison

Just enough room to talk about M. John Harrison's tale of watery supernatural goings on in a near future England, where misfits and outsiders Shaw and Victoria lurch from crisis to crisis. Shaw is out of work and out for friends when he bumps into his future employer, Tom, who turns out to be his noisy neighbour and who draws Shaw into his weirdness. Victoria, Shaw's on/off girlfriend, uproots to the Midlands to take over her late mother's house and meets people old, young and bizarre. Both of these characters drift though their own despair and aimlessness, mirrored in the disintegration of the land and people surrounding them. Harrison's an old hand at science fiction and this novel will surely please his fans. It wears its speculative fiction credentials lightly, though, and is surely too British a novel to travel too far overseas. I liked its gentle characterization and odd story beats but I yearned for more pace and more relatable protagonists.

MB